D0908119

SHADOW OF THE GUN

SHADOW OF THE GUN

A WESTERN DUO

LEWIS B. PATTEN

FIVE STAR

An imprint of Thomson Gale, a part of The Thomson Corporation

THOMSON

GALE

Detroit • New York • San Francisco • New Haven, Conn. • Waterville, Maine • London

THOMSON
GALE

Thomson Gale is part of The Thomson Corporation.

Thomson and Star Logo and Five Star are trademarks and Gale is a registered trademark used herein under license.

Set in 11 pt. Plantin.

LIBRARY OF CONGRESS CATALOGING-IN-PUBLICATION DATA

Patten, Lewis B.
  [Killing]
  Shadow of the gun : a western duo / by Lewis B. Patten. — 1st ed.
    p. cm. — (A Five Star Western)
  ISBN-13: 978-1-59414-563-6 (alk. paper)
  ISBN-10: 1-59414-563-6 (alk. paper)
  I. Patten, Lewis B. Shadow of the gun. II. Title.
PS3566.A79K44 2007
813'.54—dc22
                                                                    2007011874

First Edition. First Printing: August 2007.

Published in 2007 in conjunction with Golden West Literary Agency.

Printed in the United States of America on permanent paper
10 9 8 7 6 5 4 3 2 1

CONTENTS

★ ★ ★ ★ ★

THE KILLING

★ ★ ★ ★ ★

I

They sat like a pair of strangers, side-by-side on the buckboard's seat, and behind, bracing himself with hands against the sideboards, the boy watched them with eyes that betrayed, of all his feelings, only uncertainty.

The old man, Guy Coulter, sat on the left. His nose was like the beak of a hawk, his mouth tight-lipped and cold. His eyes, almost the color of this blazing, brassy sky, were narrowed against the glare, or perhaps they were narrowed by his bitter, angry thoughts that allowed no room for sadness.

The boy turned his head, stared at the cloud of fine dust that lay behind the light vehicle, dust that dripped from its steel-rimmed tires like water. It coated his face, his hair. It was in his mouth, gritty between his teeth.

Dust and heat, and a brassy, cloudless sky. The creekbed twisted along over on the right, damp in spots, a stagnant pool here and there along its course. But no running water. No murmuring cool water. And no fish, except the dead ones that made their stench along the dry course of the stream.

The boy's brother Knox drove, the reins held loosely and easily in his big, capable hands. Knox looked like Rudy, Rudy who was dead, who had been shot to death last night by Arch Dorrance.

Knox wasn't talking. But every so often he would glance aside at the rock-hard set of the old man's features. And once in a while he'd look back at the boy and try to reassure him with his eyes.

The boy's name was Dave, and he was ten. Right now, he was puzzled and scared, and perhaps resentful because Guy and Knox were so dog-goned evasive about why Arch had shot Rudy.

Dave stared at the ocean of gray-green sagebrush, at the dry-brown serviceberry on the slides below the rims. He stared at the fringe of spruce on the mesa tops. But he always wound up with his eyes on the cloudless sky in which the sun hung like a molten ball of merciless fire.

The old man broke the silence, saying harshly: "I sent word to Karl Freitag that he'd better have Arch Dorrance in jail when I got there. And, by heaven, he'd better have him, too!"

The boy was fiercely proud of his father in that instant, proud of his implacability, proud because now he was sure Rudy's death would not go unavenged. But Knox's answering tone destroyed his surety.

Knox asked: "And then what?"

"Why, blame it, try him and convict him, that's what. He killed Rudy, didn't he?"

Knox's answer deepened Dave's confusion. "I guess maybe I'd have done the same thing. I guess you would have, too. A man's got the right. . . ."

The old man interrupted savagely: "That situation would never have come up with me. Your mother. . . ."

Knox said: "Face it, Guy. Rudy had faults. You know he was irresponsible when it came to women."

The old man made a visible effort to hold onto himself, but his face gave him away. Blue veins throbbed beneath the parched, tight-stretched brown skin of his forehead. Blood gave his face a ruddy, overheated look. His eyes were bits of ice. "Arch didn't have to kill Rudy. No, sir! He could have whipped Rudy with his fists. He didn't have to take a gun to him."

They rode in silence then, and the buckboard put the miles behind. This much Dave was beginning to realize. Rudy had done something to Arch Dorrance, and Arch had killed him for it. Rudy, who Dave had adored. The trouble had something to do with women. The freckles on Dave's nose showed dark and plain because he was so pale.

Gradually they approached the town of Chimney Rock, at the confluence of Wild Horse Creek and Grand River.

They entered town at the upper end, passed the schoolhouse, drove beneath the spreading arms of the giant cottonwoods and so came into the business district.

Guy rode with his eyes straight ahead, holding his head, high and defiant. Knox seemed to be trying awfully hard to act naturally, but it didn't quite come off. Even Dave could sense the difference, which lay in the way the townspeople looked at you, averting their glances almost instantly before you could smile or wave or say hello. It was almost as though Dave and Guy and Knox had themselves done something wrong. The townfolk were grouped in small, whispering bunches, and Dave could feel their hostile glances upon his back.

Knox slapped the backs of the slowing team with the reins and whirled around the corner to head for the jail.

A block off Main it was, a low, square building with thick, adobe walls and steel bars at the windows. Knox drew the team to a halt and Dave jumped down to tie them. He followed Knox inside, not missing the self-conscious, drifting crowd that tried to remain inconspicuous as they approached along the dusty street from Main.

Guy's first words to the sheriff were harsh and to the point: "You got him, Karl?"

Karl Freitag got up from behind his desk, with but a short glance for Knox and Dave. "Yeah, Guy. I got him. But. . . ."

"But nothin'! He killed Rudy, didn't he? You got laws ag'in' killin', ain't you? I want him tried for murder."

Freitag sighed. He was a big man, bigger than Knox. He was so big that his clothes always seemed too tight. He was heavy-browed and black of eye. He wore a long, flowing mustache that Dave greatly admired, and a dark blue shirt with a rim of sweat beneath the armpits. He said pleasantly: "Guy, hang it, you won't get a jury to convict him. You're wasting your time."

Guy's tone was cold, clipped, a tone that Dave knew and that made him scared as though he had done something bad himself. Guy said: "Suppose you do your duty and let me decide whether I'm wasting my time or not."

Freitag nodded soberly, resignedly. "All right, Guy. You're calling the dance. But I'm telling you now, Arch Dorrance will be acquitted. Unwritten law. And all you'll have to show for this will be a lot of hate and hard feeling."

Guy said a single, obscene word.

Freitag's voice was patient. "Rudy was your son. You knew as much about him as anyone. You know Arch Dorrance's wife wasn't the first. Arch just happened to come home unexpectedly. And Arch thought a heap of Sue even if she didn't make a very good ranch woman. It weren't unnatural for Arch to blame Rudy, knowing Rudy's reputation. Arch has got a temper, a devil of a temper, and it got away from him last night. But, by Judas, I can't honestly say I blame him too much."

All three of them, Freitag, Guy, and Knox kept looking over at Dave, watching their talk some because of him.

Guy said shortly: "The circuit judge is due in Chimney Rock tomorrow, ain't he?"

Dave could tell that Guy was holding himself in.

"Yes, Guy."

"Then we'll have a trial. We'll see if Arch is guilty or not."

Knox, who had been lounging against the doorjamb, moved

aside to let his father pass through. Guy asked: "Coming, Knox?"

Knox shook his head. "I want to talk to Arch. I'll be along."

The flush of anger deepened in Guy's face, but he did not protest. Silently he went out and climbed to the buckboard seat, and Dave followed, for the first time a little ashamed of his brother Knox.

Knox watched until the buckboard went out of sight around the corner. Knox was feeling pity for Guy, regret, and a helpless anger. Rudy had been his brother. But to Knox, right was right, and a man's home was inviolate. Rudy had violated Arch Dorrance's home and been killed for doing it.

You could feel sadness and grief because Rudy was gone. But if you were fair-minded at all, you sought no revenge because Rudy had been so plainly wrong. And because Arch Dorrance had been your friend, you stood before the door that led back to the cells in the building's rear, and hesitated with your hand on the doorknob, remembering the times you had hunted with Arch, the nights at roundup camp, and the long, hot days at a branding fire. You remembered Arch, not as the man who had killed your brother, but as what he had been before that.

Karl Freitag grunted: "Go on, Knox. The door ain't locked."

Knox opened the door. Arch Dorrance sat on a bench inside his cell, with his head in his big, wide hands. He looked up as the door opened.

He was a man of short stature, but broad and thick across shoulders and chest. His work shirt was open at the throat, showing a thick mat of yellow hair on his chest. The hair on his head was thinning at the temples, and was straight and fine-textured. His eyes were gray, hard as he scowled.

Knox didn't know what to say. He stood at the bars, looking down until Arch stood up. Then, still looking down a short distance, Arch said harshly: "Damn it, what do you want? You come to gloat?"

Knox shook his head. "I don't know why I came. There's not much I can say. But I'm sorry, Arch. Sorry you killed him . . . sorry for what he did, too, I guess. Maybe I wanted to ask why you had to kill him."

Dorrance grabbed the bars and his knuckles turned white. He looked steadily at Knox. "What would you have done?"

"What you did, maybe. If I set as much store by my wife as you do. But I don't reckon that would make it right." He saw the sickness come into Arch's eyes then. Dullness. Hopelessness. Soul sickness.

He was silent, wishing he had not mentioned Sue. Arch turned away from the bars and sat down again. Not looking up, he asked: "What's Guy going to do?"

"Have you tried for murder."

Freitag broke in, defying Knox with his eyes. "Arch, he can't make it stick. There ain't a jury in Colorado that'd convict you."

"But I've got to stand trial, anyway." Arch's voice was bitter. "We've got to put on a show for the country. We've got to drag Sue through the mud." He looked up, his face twisted. "Get out of here, Knox. Get out! You and me have been friends, but that's over now. It's over!"

Knox murmured: "Is it, Arch?" He stared at him for a moment more. Then, resignedly, Knox turned and went back into the jail office. He stood at the window, looking out into the blazing, hot street, looking at the parched vegetation in the vacant lots, at the leaves of the cottonwoods, speckled brown by the drought.

Freitag spoke behind him, in a neutral tone. "It's hell, Knox. You can't change Guy, I reckon?"

Knox shook his head. "Never changed him yet. I'm not sure I want to try."

"Yeah. But when the trial's over, then what? I don't guess Guy's much of a hand to take a licking lying down. What'll he do when the jury turns Arch loose?"

Knox shrugged. "Figure it out for yourself." He opened the door and stepped into the street. Absently he fumbled in his shirt pocket, withdrew a sack of Bull Durham and wheat-straw papers. He fashioned a cigarette with elaborate care.

Knox stood just over six feet. He was lean as a hungry lion, from wide shoulders to slim hips and long shanks beneath. He wore dusty Levi's tucked into high-topped, high-heeled boots. A dusty black Stetson sat on the back of his head, and tied to the hatband were a couple of sets of snake rattles.

His eyes were Coulter-blue eyes. Like Guy's. Like Rudy's. Like Dave's. All the Coulters had blue eyes. Knox's jaw was long, his cheek bones high and protruding. His hair was jet black. Tan him a little more, change those blue eyes to brown, and he might have been an Ute Indian.

He lit the cigarette and walked slowly toward town, heading for the Hazeltree Feed Store and Funeral Parlor, where Rudy's body was.

A morose depression dominated his thoughts.

II

As Guy pulled the team to a halt before Hazeltree's, he said: "Tie the team and wait, Dave. You're too young to go in." He climbed down and stumped up the steps. Dave felt a little cold as he thought of Rudy, lying in there. So cold and still.

He wasn't at all sure he wanted to see Rudy that way, so he was kind of glad Guy had said to wait. Dave admitted now that he'd dreaded seeing Rudy dead. He remembered Rudy as laughing and irresponsible, and alive.

The stares of the people along Main, the furtive stares, made him nervous, so he turned and walked down toward the river at the lower end of the street.

Down here, like up along Wild Horse Creek, the air was heavy with the smell of death. You'd think a river as big as Grand River, coming hundreds of miles from the peaks of the Divide, would have more water in it now in spite of the drought. But it was only a trickle, a thin stream no more than ten feet wide, winding back and forth in a riverbed meant for 100 times that much.

The heat, the sight of the river, the smell of dead fish, all of these things and the strain of the day became suddenly too much for Dave. He sat down on the riverbank and began to cry.

It seemed a long time that he sat there. The tears went away, and he walked down to the water and washed his face. Then he started back toward town, shamed because he had cried, and glad no one had seen him.

Three boys came shuffling across a weed-grown lot and intercepted him a dozen yards short of the town's first ramshackle building. One was Ben Freitag, the sheriff's son. Another was Orvie Gartrell's little brother Pete. The third was Willie Surdan, who was thirteen and the biggest of them all.

They blocked his path, staring at him with self-conscious and uncertain hostility. Dave stopped, and stared back. Yesterday they'd have been glad to see him, would have chattered at him like squirrels. Today it was different. Willie, always the leader, said: "Pa says your old brother Rudy got what was comin' to him. He says it's time the Coulters quit bein' so all-fired big-gety."

Pete Gartrell, too, repeated the words he had heard at home. "They'll turn Arch Dorrance loose. Likely they'll thank him fer riddin' the country of a skunk."

Willie's words had caught Dave by surprise. But the word "skunk," applied to Rudy, touched off a fierce, wild wave of rage. He launched himself at Pete, fists flying. Willie put out a foot, and Dave went to his knees in the dust.

All three of them piled onto him, pounding, kicking, biting. Again the tears came to Dave's eyes, but these were different tears. They were tears of fury.

His fist smashed into Pete's mouth, and the teeth skinned his knuckles. He elbowed Willie in the stomach, and drew a sharp gasp of pain from the older boy. The blows that *thudded* into Dave's face went unnoticed, unfelt. His arms flailed, his legs strained as he tried to free himself.

Then Willie got astraddle of his chest, and Pete held down his legs. Ben Freitag held his hands, and Willie began to pound his face. Their eyes were wild, their mouths cruelly grinning. Dave rolled his head to escape Willie's hard-pounding fists. He strained and he writhed, but there was no getting away. Their weight and their strength were too much for him.

Dave stopped crying, and a hard core of hatred began to grow in his heart.

Then a hand reached down and pulled Willie off him. The hand cuffed Willie across the mouth, and Willie slinked away across the lot. The other two turned loose, and Dave struggled to his feet, covered with dust and blood, shaking like a new calf on a cold March day.

Orvie Gartrell asked: "Hurt, Dave?"

Dave only gave him a hating, angry stare, and marched away.

Hazeltree's was a long, frame building with a wooden awning that stretched out over the walk. In ordinary times, there was always a pile of baled hay as high as a man's head on the walk against the front wall. Today, there was none. Hay was a rarity in Chimney Rock this year.

One side of the building housed the feed store, the other Hazeltree's funeral parlor. Knox Coulter climbed the three steps from the street to the walk and went into the cool, dim mustiness of its interior.

He saw Guy at once, hat in hand, standing beside the sheet-draped body of his son. Knox went over and stood at his shoulder, looking down.

Rudy was pale. But he didn't look dead. He looked as though he might be sleeping. Knox waited a decent interval, then turned, walked to the window, and began to make another cigarette.

Guy came to stand beside him, his face gray and lined, but filled with cold determination. Guy whispered: "If the jury don't hang Arch, then Dollar will."

Knox shook his head. "Let the jury decide Arch's guilt. They'll decide Rudy's while they're at it." Because he knew his words could start a bitter argument, he put a hand on Guy's shoulder, murmured—"See you."—and went quickly outside.

Knox paused on the walk, put his shoulder point against one of the awning supports, and lit the cigarette he had made. He wanted a drink. He wanted people around him and he wanted to talk. But the town's hostility made that impossible.

Downstreet, he saw Dave marching defiantly toward him from the direction of the river. His glance fell away, then returned with startled suddenness. Dave had been fighting.

Knox stepped into the street and walked toward his younger brother. Dave's face was bloody and bruised, streaked with mud and tears. His clothes were dusty and torn. Knox saw at once that Dave was on the ragged edge of breaking down. He said: "I've been looking for you. Let's go visit Nell a while."

Anger was building in Knox. Anger at the people of the town who seemed to insist on making more of this than it already was. Anger at Guy for threatening to hang Arch if the court didn't. Anger because it was all hurting Dave, because Dave didn't deserve to be hurt.

Walking, he looked down at Dave, gauged the control that

had slowly come to his brother, and asked: "Trouble?"

Dave nodded, biting his lip.

"What about?"

"Rudy." The lower lip was quivering. Knox threw his cigarette down and stepped on it from habit that was drought born and bred. He held his silence as they walked north along a shaded side street.

The DeAndrea house was a rambling, one-story frame, surrounded in front by a picket fence that needed paint. The lawn, usually so green, was brown and dry and dusty. Flowers that Nell DeAndrea had planted and cultivated were dying for lack of water.

His boots and Dave's sounded hollowly on the porch. Through the curtained window, Knox saw Nell get up from a chair. She opened the door, quickly smiling with pleasure at seeing Knox again. But her smile faded as she looked at Dave, became startled and pitying.

"Dave! What happened to you?"

"Fight," Knox said. "Can he wash up here?"

"Of course he can. Come in, both of you."

She wore a dress of red-checked gingham, its tight bodice revealing her full, young figure. Knox took off his hat, batted it once against his thigh, and followed Dave into the cool, dim parlor of the DeAndrea house.

Nell said softly: "Sit down, Knox. I'll get Dave a pan of water, and then I'll make some lemonade."

Dave sent Knox an embarrassed look, then followed her. Knox watched her slim, lithe, womanly figure as she walked toward the kitchen. Her hair was pale yellow, done in a neat bun on her neck. Her skin was white, untouched by the harsh sun and wind of this land. Her eyes were wide-set, varying between green and hazel according to her mood. A stormy girl, but one who could be restful, too.

The tight core of tension in Knox's brain began slowly to relax. This heat brought tension to men, and the drought made it worse. Your temper grew short; your reasonableness disappeared.

Knox wished he could rid himself of the odd and unaccustomed feeling of uneasiness. Yet he knew that the country and the country's people were like dry, dead grass, waiting for a single spark to start the blaze that could sweep the land and destroy them all. Animosities that might otherwise have remained hidden, grievances that might have been forgotten, would flare, not wholly because of Rudy's death, but because the drought had stolen patience and forbearance from people's minds.

Nell came back with a frosty pitcher and three glasses. Ice tinkled as she poured them full. She smiled. "The ice is almost gone. Dad put down nothing smaller than hundred-pound cakes, but I can carry the largest of them in one hand now."

Knox sipped the lemonade. Nell's smile slowly faded and at last she said: "I'm sorry about Rudy, Knox. It was a terrible thing. I hope they. . . ."

"You hope they what, Nell?"

"Why, punish Arch Dorrance, of course. What else?"

"What do you think they should do to Arch?" Knox's voice was quiet.

Nell's expression became guarded. She studied Knox a moment before she replied. At last she asked: "What do you want me to say, Knox?"

Knox tried to stifle his own impatience, but knew he failed. "Try saying what you believe, Nell. Is it that Arch should be hung for killing Rudy?"

"You're being unpleasant, Knox." A certain coldness crept into her eyes.

"I guess I am, Nell. Hang it, I feel unpleasant. I'm sorry."

Her coldness disappeared. She sat down and took his hand. "Knox," she murmured, blushing a little, "no one has ever questioned a man's being justified killing another man he catches with his wife. But that still doesn't make it right. The Bible says . . . 'Thou shalt not kill.' It doesn't say . . . 'Thou shalt not kill unless provoked.' Arch was wrong in killing Rudy no matter what the jury will have to say about it."

"But you think they'll acquit him?"

"Of course they will."

Knox scowled. "Guy isn't going to like that."

"What can he do?"

Knox made a low, mirthless chuckle. "Plenty. He can do plenty. He'll do it, too."

For a time, Nell was silent.

Knox could hear Dave as the boy emptied the wash pan on the back stoop and hung up the pan.

Nell said: "Dave's paying, too, isn't he? Oh, why do people have to be the way they are? Why does everybody, even the children, have to jump in and take sides?"

Knox shrugged. Dave came in, the dust brushed from his clothes, the blood and dirt washed from his face. He drank the cold lemonade in a few quick gulps. Knox got up, and pushed Dave toward the door.

He smiled his thanks at Nell, and she said: "Knox, don't torture yourself worrying about this. The thing is done, and no more of your doing than it was Dave's."

"All right, Nell. I'll try that."

"Where are you going now?"

"Back to Dollar with Dave. I'd as soon Guy doesn't see him tonight."

"Are you sure that's the reason?"

Knox grinned with self-derision. "Not all of it, I guess. Maybe it's partly because I don't want to have to sit on a fence for all

21

the town to see. People are funny. If you stand solidly on one side or the other, they respect you, even if you're wrong. But they've got no use for a man who can't make up his mind. I'm going home to Dollar until I get my mind made up."

"Perhaps there's some wrong on both sides of this question. Arch was surely wrong in killing Rudy, just as Rudy was wrong for doing what he did. It's no crime to be able to see both sides of a question."

Knox's grin had faded. His lips were somber, thinned out, and the worry creases had returned to his forehead. "Try telling Guy that, Nell. Try telling it to Arch, and Arch's friends."

He touched her cheek with the forefinger of his right hand, turned, and went out the door, feeling her steady gaze on his back.

But he didn't turn. He said gruffly—"Come on, Dave."—and headed for Orvie Gartrell's livery stable, where he could hire horses for both Dave and himself, thus leaving the buckboard for Guy.

Sue Dorrance had been alone all day. She had been alone most of the night as well. In the small hours of the morning, Arch had loaded Rudy Coulter's body onto a horse and had set out for Chimney Rock with no parting words for her, harsh or otherwise.

She had not slept. During the dark hours, she sat in the porch rocker, staring somberly at nothing. Later, as the sun came up to beat its heat upon her, she got up and went into the house.

She was stunned with shock, with shame, with remorse. She thought of Rudy Coulter a dozen times, dead now because she'd not had the strength to resist his advances. She thought of Arch, big, intolerant, harsh-tempered Arch. She tried to remember Arch as he had been two years ago when they were first married. But that had been a long time ago and Arch had changed.

Oddly she gave no consideration to the other people of Chimney Rock and the surrounding country. She thought only in terms of Rudy, of Arch, and of what she had done to them both.

The whole thing had begun innocently enough—Arch gone one morning a couple of months ago—Rudy riding in, hailing the house, and wanting to know where Arch was.

Sue made her first mistake then—patting her hair into place, smoothing her dress, stepping outside, and making her smile unnecessarily bright. A woman dissatisfied with her life, with her husband's new coldness, smiling up at a man who had the money, the power and position that her husband, she knew by then, would never achieve.

He'd smiled back at her, pleased at her warmth, experienced in these things and sensing perhaps that she would be an easy conquest if handled skillfully.

Arch had not mattered to him, or Sue, or his own family. He was like many men, shedding honor like a cloak where a woman was concerned.

She had asked him to dismount, to come in for a cup of coffee, and he had accepted. They had talked about Arch, about the drought and the scarcity of grass and water, about everything except the thing uppermost in both their minds. But both of them knew. Sue had known and Rudy had known.

Sitting here, remembering, Sue's mind suddenly cried: *It was Arch's fault, too! He was always finding fault, growing colder toward me every day. He was always going to town, drinking, coming home late at night, scowling and mean-tempered.*

Perhaps Sue was not always honest with Arch. Perhaps no one is wholly honest at all times with all people. But Sue was honest with herself. She admitted now that Arch's coldness, his ragged temper, his drinking, all these things had been a result not a cause. They had been the result of Sue's dissatisfaction, which Arch had not failed to see.

During the drought, when hay stopped growing, when grass dried up, when cattle began to die, Arch had deserved something better from her than dissatisfaction. For they'd both seen the drought as an enemy that could only aggravate the cause of their trouble.

"He never should have married me!" she cried aloud. "And I should have known that this kind of life would never suit me."

Which brought her mind back to Rudy. Obscurely, deep inside, she'd encouraged Rudy as a subconscious revenge against Arch for his neglect. She would, in the course of her conversation, talk about Arch sometimes, saying plaintively: "Arch leaves me alone so much. He's gone today. He was gone last Monday. And he'll be gone Saturday."

Giving Rudy his cue, which Rudy never missed. Saturday he'd come riding in, observing the formality of asking: "Arch home, Sue?" She would return his mocking smile, and he'd get down and come in.

Rudy was careful, and expert. He didn't push himself, which might have scared her off. He let her know what was in his mind by glance and smile and sly innuendo. He left it up to her from there on.

That was like Rudy. That was the sop to his conscience, what little conscience was left to him.

So Sue herself made the first move, throwing herself into his arms as he was leaving one day, begging: "Rudy! For heaven's sake, Rudy, stop tormenting me!"

Remembering this, Sue's face flamed with shame. He'd forced her to make the initial overture, and of course then there could be no backing out. He'd refused to permit it.

So it had gone on—and on.

Sue had truly loved him. There was no denying it. Yet there could be no excuse for their furtiveness, for continuing the affair behind Arch's back.

Sue had at first insisted that they tell Arch, that she leave him and marry Rudy as soon as it was possible. Rudy had effectively halted that by coldness, by failure to come on the days he was supposed to come. And Sue, wildly in love by now, had no choice but to take Rudy on his own terms or not at all.

She paced the floor; she dropped her face into her hands and wept. She condemned herself bitterly and without mercy.

Nothing helped to ease her guilt, her remorse.

Arch was probably jailed, surely accused of murder. But he would get out. He would be acquitted. And after that?

Sue knew what would happen after that. She would leave. Arch would insist upon it, since it was the only possible solution. Living in the Chimney Rock country would be out of the question. Her shame would be public knowledge. Every man and woman in the country would condemn her. She would be a pariah, an outcast. Even if Arch consented to keeping her, which he surely would not.

Left, then, was but one alternative. Flight.

With something to do now, she got up, hurried to the bedroom, and began to pack. It was in packing that she found the gun Arch had used on Rudy, lying on the floor where he had flung it.

She picked it up, stared at it with horror and dawning fear. She began to laugh, hysterically, wildly. What could be more fitting than that the gun that had taken the life of the guilty man should also take the life of the guilty woman? What could be more fitting?

Ice in her veins killed Sue's laughter. She placed the gun against her breast and thumbed back the hammer.

III

Knox Coulter never knew exactly what it was that turned him in at Arch's gate. An impulse, perhaps, obscure and unthinking. He said: "Dave, stay here a minute."

Going down the lane, though, he considered his action and knew that he wanted to talk to Sue, wanted to find out exactly what had happened last night, what her feelings had been toward Rudy.

He was aware that he could not resolve the turmoil in himself on the facts he knew. He needed more facts, and Sue was the only one from whom he could get them. Rudy could not give them to him. Arch wouldn't. So only Sue was left.

Knox had admitted, all day, the possibility that Arch had jumped to an unwarranted conclusion. Arch was normally hot-tempered and precipitous in his actions. The drought and the worry it had caused had probably increased this tendency in him. So it was entirely possible that the connection between Rudy and Sue had been an imagined one, a product of Arch's thinking and touchy temper.

Arch's house was a three-room affair, constructed of logs and chinked with mud on the outside. Inside, it was finished, plastered, and papered with bright paper. Arch had worked hard on the house, trying to make up to Sue for what she would miss leaving town.

Knox knocked hesitantly, for he did not know how he would be received. Utter silence within the house answered his knock, so he knocked again and, still receiving no answer, opened the door and went in. He called: "Sue! You home?"

The house was untidy. Papers and magazines lay scattered about, and clothes. He walked through the parlor and went into the kitchen.

He returned to the parlor and started for the door. And then he heard a small, slight noise from the bedroom. He called again: "Sue? You there?"

He got no answer, save for a sharply indrawn breath. Embarrassed acutely, he crossed to the bedroom door and stepped inside.

What he saw froze him instantly. Sue stood by the window, a heavy Colt .44 revolver in her hand. The muzzle rested against her left breast and the hammer was thumbed back.

She was a small woman in stature, fully rounded as a woman should be. Her hair today was untidy and uncombed, her face pale and drawn. Yet even these things could not conceal the haunting beauty that was peculiarly hers. Her eyes were large, softly brown, her lips full and sensitive. At the moment, her expression was one of wildness, of unpredictability, of utter hopelessness.

She did not speak. She only stared, with surprise, with shock, at Knox Coulter. Knox said softly, persuasively: "Sue, another death won't solve anything. And it will finish Arch."

Still she stared. Her lips were bloodless, scarcely moving as she whispered: "I'm no good, Knox. No good for myself or for Arch. This is the best way."

"It's no way at all." Knox's voice had turned harsh. He took a slow step toward her, another. Panic touched her expression and he could see the slight tightening in the muscles of her hand. He stopped. Again he made his voice persuasive. "Sue, that's a coward's way. Everybody makes mistakes. But they don't have to be final. Arch still loves you."

She laughed, and the muzzle of the .44 wavered a little. Her laugh, so bitter with self-condemnation, was ringing in his ears as Knox drove toward her. His flat hand went out, slapped the gun away. The hammer fell, and the gun roared. Black, acrid smoke billowed from its muzzle.

Knox seized her wrist before she could thumb back the hammer again.

He twisted savagely. The gun *clattered* to the floor. And the restraint went out of Sue. All through the night, all through the morning she had been tearless with shock. Her weeping began with a tremor in her body. Knox held her in his arms, and the flood of tears came, wracking her, tearing her apart.

Knox patted her back awkwardly. He supposed he should condemn Sue Dorrance as the rest of the country was doing. It rather surprised him that he felt no hate toward her, nor even blame. More or less neutral, his mind neither condoned nor condemned the thing she had done. She was simply a person, stricken with grief and remorse, who now needed help.

Gradually her sobbing subsided. Knox asked: "Have you had anything to eat?"

She shook her head mutely. He made a thin smile. "Wash your face. Comb your hair. Put on a clean dress. I'll stir up some breakfast for you."

He released her, picked up the .44, and stuffed it down into his belt.

It was no particular chore for Knox to set the kitchen to rights, build a fire in the stove, and put on coffee pot and frying pan. Nor did it bother him to collect the dirty dishes and begin to wash them. Knox had been raised around bunkhouses and cow camps, and in cattle country these tasks are not peculiarly women's tasks.

He was almost finished when Sue came into the kitchen. Her face showed a little color from the scrubbing she had given it. Her hair was neatly brushed. And she wore a fresh gingham dress.

Knox nodded toward the kitchen table and she sank down into a chair. He set a plate before her, a plate loaded with eggs and bacon, and poured her a cup of coffee. He poured himself a cup, too, and sat down across from her.

She smiled at him wearily. "What now?" But she began to

eat, a healthy sign, Knox decided.

He didn't try to deceive her. "The worst is still to come."

"The trial?"

He nodded. "Guy insisted on a trial. Otherwise, there needn't have been one. You'll be called on to testify, because they'll have to know if Arch was justified in killing Rudy."

She shuddered, and her face paled. "When is the trial to be?"

"Tomorrow, I guess. The circuit judge is due in Chimney Rock tomorrow. A murder trial would naturally have priority, so I guess it'll come first." He sipped the scalding coffee, watching Sue.

She ate without relish, but with obvious determination. Knox's mind kept saying: *But for her, Rudy would be alive. I ought to hate her.*

She must have divined his thoughts, for she asked: "Why don't you hate me, Knox?"

He grinned wryly. "Maybe because I knew Rudy so well. This may come as a shock to you, Sue, but you weren't the first. Women were a game to Rudy, and he didn't like playing for keeps. It was only a matter of time until someone would get Rudy. It happened to be Arch, that's all."

He got up and reached for his hat, wanting to ask the question he had come to ask, yet very reluctant to. He said: "Will you be all right now? No more foolishness?"

She shook her head.

Knox blurted: "Sue, was Arch . . ."—he halted, clenched his jaws briefly, and went on—"was Arch justified? I've got to know."

Her voice was hardly audible. But her glance was unwavering. "I'm afraid he was."

Knox felt himself flushing. He muttered: "You get some sleep. Is there anything you need?"

She ignored that. As though the need to justify herself in Knox's eyes were a desperate thing with her, she cried: "Knox, you've got to believe this! I loved Rudy. I wanted to tell Arch about us, but. . . ." Her eyes glistened with unshed tears.

Knox laughed bitterly. "Sure. But Rudy wouldn't let you. Rudy didn't want any woman for keeps. So stop worrying about Rudy. He was my brother, but that doesn't mean I have to approve of all the stinking things he did. You get some sleep now."

He went outside and mounted his horse, still with the Colt .44 stuffed down into his belt. He hoped the urge for self-destruction was gone from Sue. But you never knew. You never knew.

Dave had come halfway down the lane, drawn by the sound of the shot, but hesitant and uncertain. He asked shakily: "Knox, you all right?"

"Sure, kid. Why?"

"I heard a shot."

Knox murmured, "An accident. A mistake is all." He was silent for a moment, watching Dave. He said finally: "Dave, there's some things that're best not talked about. One is that shot. Another is us stopping here. You reckon you can keep still about them?"

"Sure, Knox."

"All right. Let's go home."

Past noon now, and the day was blistering hot. Hot and dry. Already the sky was beginning to take on that strangely brassy glare that Knox had grown so used to this year.

Leaving the road, they angled over toward the creek, through sagebrush that was withers high on their horses.

Dave rode ten or fifteen feet behind Knox, squinting against the glare. Suddenly Knox's horse shied violently, and he heard the dry, brittle rattle of a snake. He hauled up on the reins, yanked out the .44. The horse wouldn't stand, so Knox swung down.

The snake was coiled not two feet from the deep imprints of

the horse's hoofs. Knox shot and the snake's head disappeared.

His horse had wandered off. Knox shoved the gun back into his belt and walked toward him. He heard the brush rustle fifty feet away and turned curiously.

His own tenseness surprised him, as did the fact that his hand automatically sought the grips of the .44. He grinned ruefully, seeing Joe Ryecroft—Diamondback Joe as he was called—coming at a slow shuffle through the brush. Joe looked down at the snake, stooped, and cut off the rattles. He stood then, saying: "Howdy, Dave. Hello, Knox."

Knox nodded, waiting with quiet patience. Diamondback Joe was a small man, withered and wrinkled as a dry apple. From constant exposure to sun and elements, his skin was like brown, cracked saddle leather. His eyes, blue and surrounded by crow's-foot wrinkles, were tiny and set close together. His thin lips held a knowing smile.

If you didn't know about Joe, he'd startle you. His hatband was made up of a solid, clustered string of rattlesnake rattles. There must have been 200 or 300 of them, Knox guessed.

Joe asked, his voice high and reedy: "Been visitin', son?"

"Might call it that." Knox's voice was clipped, short.

Joe looked at Dave. "Bet Knox told you not to say nothin' about that visit, didn't he, Dave?"

Dave looked inquiringly at Knox. Knox scowled. Hang the old snooper anyway. If there was ever anything you didn't want seen or known, Diamondback Joe was sure to be poking around the neighborhood. And his old eyes didn't miss much.

"You an' Rudy ain't much alike, some ways." The statement was a hint, a hint for more information.

Knox said: "Rudy's dead. Arch shot him last night."

"Ain't surprisin'. Ain't surprisin' at all. Man sees a lot, does he keep his eyes open."

"And you do." Knox grinned at him without humor.

"Generally keep my mouth shut, though." Joe grinned back.

Knox felt as though he had been put on the defensive. He opened his mouth to explain, then clamped it shut angrily. He was damned if he'd explain anything to Diamondback Joe. It was none of Joe's business.

So Knox changed the subject. "Snake hunting good?"

"Passable." Joe turned and stared at the snake Knox had killed. Dead, it was as ugly as it had been alive, although perhaps not so fearsome. It still twitched, even with its head and rattles gone. It was big as rattlers went, over five feet long. Joe said: "Queer how often a man hits a snake's head when he shoots. Know what I think about that?"

"What?"

"I figger the snake strikes at the bullet. A rattler's fast, man. Faster'n lightning. Maybe faster'n a bullet."

Knox found that hard to believe. Still, if anyone would know, Diamondback Joe would. Knox caught up his horse and mounted. He murmured: "Maybe so, Joe. Maybe so."

Knox reined around, but Joe's voice stopped him. "You reckon they'll be a trial?"

Knox nodded. "Tomorrow."

"Arch'll get off." It was a statement.

Knox nodded again.

Joe was grinning, a funny little wicked grin. "Trouble then, hey? Give Guy an excuse to do what he's been itchin' to do all summer."

"What's that?" Knox knew, but he wanted to hear Joe put it into words, to know that it wasn't all in his own mind.

"Run 'em out. Run every blamed one of 'em out. Arch first. Then the others. Take their grass, take their water. You ain't dumb, son. You know what'll happen just as good as I do."

Knox nodded reluctantly. "Guess I do at that."

"And where'll you be? You're friends with Arch, or useta be.

You're friends with some of the others, too. You went to school with some of 'em. Where'll you be, Knox?"

"You talk too much," Knox said sourly, and rode away, not looking back.

Behind him, Joe kept cackling: "You'll be right in the middle, son. Smack dab in the middle. That's where you're a-goin' to be."

And Knox guessed he was right.

Riding, with Dave so silent behind him, Knox could feel his anger rising. He found it centered mostly on simple, aged Diamondback Joe Ryecroft, which he immediately admitted was unfair. Joe had simply put into words Knox Coulter's own thoughts, and could hardly be blamed for that. And because Knox didn't want to think about the trouble that was shaping, he thought about Diamondback Joe.

Dave asked: "How come Joe hates snakes so much, Knox?"

Knox reined in a little, allowing Dave to come abreast. He said: "He's an old-timer, Dave. Used to have a wife. She was a real nice woman, kind of tiny and smiling. I remember, when I was about your age, we'd go by there sometimes on the way home from school. She'd always have a jar of fresh-baked cookies and cool milk for us. One day she was pulling carrots in her garden and a snake bit her on the wrist."

"Gee!"

Knox went on: "Folks don't always die of snakebite. But Joe's wife was frail, and there weren't any help around for her when it happened. Joe came in from irrigating and found her dead, swelled up and purple from the poison, hardly looking at all like the woman he remembered. I guess something snapped in Joe's mind. He brooded around for a couple of months, letting his place go to seed, going to seed himself. And then he changed. He made snake hunting a kind of personal crusade, as though some way he could avenge his wife's death by killing every rattler he could find. Folks got to calling him Diamondback Joe."

Dave whistled. "Gosh."

"They thought he was touched, and maybe he was. But his mind isn't gone, by any means." Knox wondered if Diamondback Joe would talk, if he would tell that he had seen Knox Coulter coming out of Arch's house. If he did, he would manage to complicate matters further that were already complicated enough.

They reached the creek, watered their horses in a bad-smelling pool, then spurred upcountry in the direction of Dollar.

IV

News has a way of traveling in the range country. By word of mouth it goes, yet with a rapidity that is sometimes amazing.

When Knox rode out of Dollar early next morning, he could see the dust over the long stretch of road ahead, dust stirred up by the passing of buckboards and horsemen. All the country would be present at Arch Dorrance's trial.

Had Guy been home, he would have ordered every hand on Dollar into the saddle for the trip to town. Yet Knox knew that Dollar, riding into Chimney Rock in a body, would have the effect of a red flag waved in a bull's face. To the people of Chimney Rock, and to Arch Dorrance's neighbors, it would be a challenge, one that could not be ignored. It might even result in the flare of violence before the day was done.

So he ordered them all to stay home, save for Dollar's foreman, Red Daly. From Dave on up, they grumbled and complained at the order. And Knox was not even sure they would obey, feeling as they did that old Guy would countermand Knox's orders if he were around.

Dollar Ranch covered the valley of a tributary of Wild Horse Creek known as Dollar Creek, from its mouth to its source, a distance of nearly thirty miles. Dollar claimed for its range the entire top of Dry Ridge, to the south of the valley. The other ridge, known as Wild Horse Ridge, was claimed and used by the smaller ranchers that inhabited the valley of Wild Horse Creek.

Dry Ridge, true to its name, was drier than Wild Horse Ridge. Its water holes were mostly dried up now, save for two down on the point, and three farther back. Last time Guy had come back from riding the ridge, he had predicted that they would all be dry within thirty days. That would leave Dollar in desperate straits.

Wild Horse Ridge, on the other hand, had plenty of water, even now. The grass was a good deal thinner because there was a lot more timber. Yet perhaps it was this very abundance of timber that prevented the springs on Wild Horse Ridge from drying up. So the war, when it began, would be over Wild Horse Ridge.

Daly, a small, wizened but muscular man, murmured as they passed through the gate: "Knox, you know what you're doing, leaving the crew to home?"

"I know what I'm trying to do."

"And what's that?" Daly's face was red from the sun, and it never seemed to tan. Everything about Red Daly was red, his face, his thinning hair, his hands; even the whites of his eyes were bloodshot red from the ever-present sun glare.

Knox said: "Keep trouble from flaring up until Guy's had time to cool off some. Arch is going to be turned loose, and Guy's going to be pretty hot about that. If the crew's in town, anything can happen because the town will resent their presence. It will look like Dollar's trying to intimidate the court."

"You reckon Guy will cool off?"

"Red," Knox said disgustedly, "I don't know. Maybe this business will be just an excuse to him, an excuse to move in on Wild Horse Ridge. But the devil. . . ." He stopped, not quite knowing how to phrase his thought.

Red grinned, looking a little like Diamondback Joe when he did. "I know, Knox. It's like Guy to be grabby but it ain't like him to skirt around somethin'."

"No. It isn't. There hasn't been much trouble around here since I've been big enough to know what's going on. But I've heard the stories. Guy's always taken what he wanted without needing any more excuse than just that he wanted it. Needing a phony excuse like this looks like a sign of weakness."

"That's just what the rest of the country's goin' to think."

Knox only grunted his assent. The sun crawled higher in the sky, beating down with increasing intensity. The miles slowly dropped behind, and frequently Knox and Daly would ride from the road to the creek to water and cool their horses for a few moments there in the shade. Water them from one of the dwindling pools.

Knox said once: "Lord! You'd think it would rain sometime."

"Yeah. But it won't."

Knox could feel his irritability rising. This was the way it was going to be in town today. Everyone, judge, sheriff, townspeople, those from Dollar and from the smaller ranches on Wild Horse Creek, all of them would be irritable and touchy.

They reached Wild Horse Creek, and turned south toward Chimney Rock. It was nearly 10:00 when they came into town, two dusty, sweating horsemen, with faces overly red from the heat.

The courthouse stood surrounded by brownish cottonwoods a block and a half off Main. Buckboards and buggies and saddle horses were clustered before it. Knox rode under a cottonwood and dismounted just as the sheriff, Karl Freitag, came up the street with Arch beside him.

Arch was handcuffed to Karl, an unnecessary precaution, of course. And Knox knew it instantly for what it was. Karl's reluctance to offend Guy.

Arch met Knox's glance as he went past, and quickly looked away. Knox scowled, unreasonably angered by this. A buggy pulled up, and one of Freitag's deputies handed Sue Dorrance down and walked with her into the courthouse. A teenage boy got into the buggy and drove it away toward the stable.

Daly said: "Wonder where Guy is."

Knox shrugged. "I don't know. But we've got ten minutes before the trial starts. I could use a beer."

"Me, too. Walk, or ride?"

"Walk," Knox said. "It isn't far."

Reilly's saloon was closest, being just a block and a half away on Main. Knox angled across to the shady side of the street, with Daly beside him.

They met Guy coming toward the courthouse. Of all those Knox had seen this morning, Guy looked the coolest. You could tell that he had just slipped into that fresh khaki shirt because it wasn't yet stained with sweat. Guy looked briefly at Knox, then at Red Daly. He asked shortly: "Where's the crew?"

Knox said: "They're home at Dollar."

Guy's color started to rise, and his brows drew together. Knox didn't want a scene here on the street. So he said: "Red and me are dry from the ride. We're going after a beer. Want to come?"

Guy shook his head. His hard, cold Coulter eyes promised Knox a later reckoning over his orders to the crew. He stalked away, heading toward the courthouse, his back straight and stiff. Knox caught Daly looking at him uneasily. Daly said: "When's the funeral to be?"

Knox didn't know. He said: "I haven't heard. Today, likely. Delay's bad in weather this hot."

"Sure."

In silence then, they finished their walk and pushed into Reilly's saloon. It began to empty as they arrived, maybe because of the time and the crowd's awareness that the trial would be starting soon. Maybe it was more than that, a reluctance to stand at the bar with these representatives of Dollar.

Knox said angrily: "Judas, it's like Dollar was on trial instead of Arch Dorrance."

Big Orvie Gartrell turned at that, put his glance on Knox, and said: "Maybe you think Dollar ain't on trial."

Knox felt the sudden rise of rashness in him that he didn't even try to control. He said softly: "On trial for what, Orvie? On trial for what?"

Orvie stepped toward him, truculent, perhaps even a little drunk. He sneered. "For thinkin' the whole Chimney Rock country is Dollar's acorn. For thinkin' that even our women belong to Dollar. For trying to tell us we better not kick up a fuss if Dollar tries to grab somethin' from us, else we'll wind up in jail or over there at the courthouse bein' tried for murder."

"You speaking just for yourself, Orvie?"

"No, by hell! They're all behind me. And you sons better not start anything when the jury turns Arch loose, neither."

Knox began to grin. "You rather I'd start it now, Orvie?"

Orvie's eyes widened with surprise, then narrowed back with wicked anticipation. Orvie stood only an inch taller than Knox. But he was heavier by thirty pounds. Heavy with muscle he had developed during a lifetime over his blacksmith's forge, shoeing horses, running his livery barn. Orvie said: "Why, come on, Knox. Come on!"

Knox knew this was foolish. So far as he knew, Orvie was a good enough sort. And he probably was speaking the mind of the country. Yet the odd rashness persisted in Knox, and the need to release the past two days' frustration in some kind of physical encounter.

He had made his challenge, and now he would stick by it. He

lunged, lashed out with his two fists at Orvie's face. His left smashed Orvie's nose, his right sank into Orvie's right eye socket.

Orvie's sudden, reflexive right caught Knox flush on the point of the jaw. Lights flashed before Knox's eyes. He was driven back, back against the bar with a crash that could have been heard in the street. He stood for a moment, shaking his head. Orvie came in, and Knox dodged, circling to get his back away from the bar. Orvie was like a big bear, flat-footed, but with pure dynamite in his fists. Knox sprang in, lashed out, and sprang back, getting away with it this time. Orvie's big fist missed him by a couple of inches.

As Knox fought, his wildness went away, and in its place came a realization that this was a fight he couldn't win. Orvie was slow, and big; Knox was fast and maybe just as tough. Knox could win the physical part of this fight. He could knock Orvie senseless. But in the eyes of the crowd, it would be just another score against Dollar.

Piled on top of that realization came another, which was that no matter what he and Guy and the Dollar crew did, they would be wrong in the eyes of the country. That simplified things for him, because what you do doesn't matter so much when you know you'll be adjudged wrong anyway.

Knox darted in, sank his left in Orvie's middle. Orvie grunted, and dropped his guard. He bent just a little from the pain in his mid-section. Knox brought up a savage right hook, with all his weight, all the force of his shoulder and back behind it.

It landed on Orvie's jaw point with a sound like the report of a pistol.

Orvie was out, or nearly so, Knox in close, his guard spread out. One of Orvie's huge fists came up with a vicious, reflexive action, and landed on the side of Knox's jaw.

They staggered away from each other, both incapable of further action. The room swam before Knox's eyes. Red Daly caught him, kept him from falling. Red said: "That's enough. Trial's starting."

Orvie hung by his elbows from the bar, his eyes glazed, dazed. But as Knox and Red turned, he said: "Another time, Knox. Another time and I'll knock your damned block off."

"Sure, Orvie. Sure." Knox followed Red Daly into the street.

Daly said: "Judas, Knox, what's the matter with people? Dollar's been bread and beans for the whole damned town as long as I can remember. The little outfits on Wild Horse Creek got their start stealing Dollar beef."

"They're scared, Red. The drought's got 'em edgy and they're scared." He scowled, walked a few moments in silence, then said softly as though thinking aloud: "And scared people are dangerous."

V

The courthouse was jam-packed, with even the standing room gone. Guy had saved a couple of seats up front for Knox and Daly. Knox sank down into the hard, uncushioned chair and put his hat on the floor between his feet. The judge rapped his gavel for order and went through the formalities of opening the session of court.

Sam DeAndrea, as county attorney, took the floor first. He was a slight man, white of hair, wearing a white, pointed beard. He said: "Your honor. Gentlemen of the jury. This is a murder trial. Two nights ago, the defendant, Arch Dorrance, shot and killed Rudy Coulter in cold blood. Coulter was unarmed. He had no chance to defend himself. Due to mitigating circumstances, the State does not seek the death penalty. The charge is second degree murder."

He called Arch to the stand. Arch was pale, but his voice was firm and strong. He told of returning home, of finding his wife in Rudy Coulter's arms.

Arch finished his testimony, after frankly admitting he had killed Rudy. DeAndrea called Sue Dorrance to the stand, and she corroborated Arch's story in its essential details.

DeAndrea made a speech that lasted fifteen minutes to the jury. He admitted that Arch had been wronged. But he repeated the words Nell had spoken to Knox: "The Bible says . . . 'Thou shalt not kill.' It doesn't say . . . 'Thou shalt not kill unless provoked.' Essentially the law says the same thing, and the laws are made for the protection of the people. Respect for law vanishes if men who take it into their own hands are allowed to go unpunished."

He rested his case, asking the jury to return a verdict of guilty as charged.

Arch's attorney, Stuart Clifton, took over from there. He harangued the jury on the sanctity of the home. He spoke at length of the "unwritten law" of a man's right to defend his home. Knox could see, before he had been talking five minutes, that he had his case won. The faces of the jury were sympathetic, in sharp contrast to their hard unfriendliness toward Sam De-Andrea.

Clifton rested his case, smiling smoothly, throwing a single triumphant glance at Guy, a glance that made three men in the jury box grin.

Knox looked at Guy, knowing instantly that Guy recognized defeat. All that remained was awaiting the verdict that could be but one thing.

The jury went out. The crowd stirred in the courtroom, talking in subdued whispers, shifting in their seats noisily.

Knox realized that he was sweating. Guy sat still, tense and cold, beside him. Guy's eyes were hard, implacable. Knox could almost see Guy's mind working, planning his revenge.

The jury stayed out ten minutes. To make it look as though there had been some debate, Knox guessed. Actually the verdict was reached before they left the courtroom. The foreman of the jury announced it in grave, measured tones: "We find the defendant, Arch Dorrance, not guilty."

Arch sat utterly still, pale and unmoving. But the courtroom burst into cheers. In less than a minute, Arch was completely hidden by those who sought to congratulate him. Guy got up, saying harshly—"Come on. Let's go."—and Knox and Red followed him out.

A man yelled: "That takes Dollar down a peg, by Judas!"

Another: "What's the matter, Guy? Did the law crawl out of Dollar's pocket?"

A laugh followed that. A mocking laugh from a dozen throats.

Guy made no sign that he had heard. But the red color of his neck deepened, and he savagely shoved a man aside that was in his way.

The jeers grew in volume, became a low, threatening roar. Karl Freitag's huge voice rose above this, yelling: "Hey now! Cut that out!" Then Guy was out of the door, with Knox and Daly following behind.

Knox knew that now was a poor time for him to question his father, yet he also knew that if something was to stem the tide of rage in Guy, it must happen soon, before that rage had time to sour. So he said: "Guy, it's over. Try to. . . ."

But Guy interrupted him coldly. "Over? Hell no, it ain't over. It's only beginning." His voice was loud, loud and clear. It was overheard by half a dozen of the people who clustered about the courthouse steps. It was overheard, as perhaps Guy intended it should be. And it served as a threat and a promise.

In the blistering heat of afternoon, a hearse drawn by four black horses pulled away from Hazeltree's, heading for the cemetery.

Behind it came a surrey, carrying Guy and Knox and Daly, and behind that a buggy bearing Sam DeAndrea, his daughter Nell, and the town's parson.

The folks of Chimney Rock watched the small procession, as did the ranchers in from Wild Horse Creek for the trial. But none of them joined it.

And so Rudy Coulter's body was buried with few but his immediate family to mourn him. His body was gone, but the trouble he had started was not. Not yet.

Jess Arnold was a bachelor. Next to Arch Dorrance, he was the largest single rancher on Wild Horse Creek. He was a little surprised when, at 9:00 on the night of the trial, Orvie Gartrell sidled up to him where he stood at the bar and said: "Jess, the sheriff'd like to talk to you an' me down at the jail for a minute."

Jess raised his black eyes and looked at Orvie suspiciously. Jess was a man gone to fat. His face was ponderous with it, sagging at neck and jowls. His eyes looked out of this mountain of flesh like a hog's and with about as much warmth. He asked: "What for?"

"Didn't say. But he said it was important."

Jess considered that. Jess didn't have much use for Freitag. No man whose life is a procession of pilferings has much use for the representatives of the law. For an instant Jess wondered what Freitag had found out.

Orvie said impatiently: "Well? You coming?"

Jess shrugged. "Sure. Why not?" He even managed a mirthless grin.

He followed Orvie outside into the hot, still night. Most of the crowd had disappeared from the streets. They'd hung around until just after dark, waiting to see if anything would happen.

But Guy and Knox and Daly had gone on back to Dollar.

Arch Dorrance had taken his wife and gone home to Wild Horse Creek. Trouble, at least for now, had apparently been postponed.

In silence, the two covered the block that lay between Main and the jail. The jail door was open, and Karl Freitag sat at his desk with his booted feet upon it. Orvie preceded Jess inside and asked: "What's on your mind, Karl?"

The sheriff looked at him uncertainly. At last he said: "I've got an idea, is all. I need some help to put it over."

Jess said suspiciously: "Why pick on us?" His expression was truculent.

Freitag grinned unpleasantly, showing his yellowed teeth. He said: "Well, I'll tell you, Jess. This job ain't exactly lawful. But it'll make us all filthy rich. I figured you'd like that."

"There's more to it than that."

"Sure." Freitag fished in his desk, drew out a handbill, and gave it to Jess. It was a Reward dodger and it had Jess Arnold's picture on it. Although yellowed with age, it was still valid. The charge was rape, and the reward offered was $500. Freitag said: "You changed your name, Jess, but a man don't change his looks."

Panic raced across Arnold's face. Freitag grinned at him. He said: "Relax, Jess. I don't intend to use this thing. It's only insurance, in a manner of speaking."

"Insurance against what?" Try as he would, Jess couldn't keep the panicked tremor out of his voice. Nor could he keep his jowls from quivering.

"Against you listening to my proposition and then spilling the beans."

"All right, I'll listen."

"Sure you will. But wait a minute." Freitag chuckled. He seemed to be enjoying himself now. All of his earlier uncertainty was gone. He turned to Orvie Gartrell. Gartrell was a pasty shade of white. Freitag said: "Scared, Orvie?"

Orvie started to bluster. But he subsided quickly enough under Freitag's unfeeling stare.

Freitag said: "We both know what you did, don't we, Orvie?"

"I don't know what you're talking about."

"Sure you do, Orvie. Sure you do."

Orvie seemed to choke. "I thought. . . ."

"You thought nobody knew about it. You were wrong, Orvie. There wasn't much fuss kicked up when that whiskey drummer disappeared. How much did he have on him, Orvie? A couple of hundred? That's peanuts to what I'm about to offer you. But you shouldn't have buried him in your backyard, Orvie. He makes evidence against you there."

Orvie, for a big man, looked pitifully small now. His big hands were sweating and he kept rubbing their palms against his pants to dry them.

Freitag said smoothly: "Let's forget about that, Orvie, shall we?"

Orvie nodded dumbly.

Jess stared at the sheriff with something akin to horror. The sheriff grinned at him. "I surprised you, didn't I, Jess? You thought I was working this damned lousy job for the fifty a month the county pays. Well, I haven't been working for that. A sheriff finds out things and, if he uses his head, turns them into money."

Jess whispered: "Blackmail."

"Sure. Blackmail. Most people will pay to keep their secrets. You'd be surprised at the people in Chimney Rock that are paying me money."

"What do you want from us?"

"You two are lucky. I don't want anything from you but your help tonight. And in return for that, you'll get a share of the profits."

The little, twitchy muscles in Jess Arnold began slowly to

relax. At least here was something a man could understand. What they were about to do was outside the law. That much was sure. And when it was done, Freitag would no longer have a hold over either of them. For he would be involved himself. Arnold said, confidently now: "All right, Sheriff. Spill it."

Freitag took his feet off the desk and leaned forward. He picked up the dodger on Jess Arnold and put it back in the desk drawer under a pile of other papers. He said: "The country's like a charge of dynamite tonight. What would it take to set it off?"

Jess said: "Not much, I guess."

Orvie was silent.

Freitag said: "Guy made his brag about what he'd do if the jury turned Arch loose. Suppose he was to do it?"

"Do what?"

Freitag said patiently: "Why, do what the court failed to do. Hang Arch."

"But he won't do that. He won't go that far. He may try to run Arch out of the country, but he won't hang him."

"Suppose he did, though? What would happen?"

Jess Arnold whistled. "Plenty would happen. Every two-bit rancher on Wild Horse Creek would be ready to ride by morning. They'd make Guy Coulter wish he'd never heard of Arch Dorrance."

"Exactly. And with Arch gone, I guess Sue'd be willing enough to sell out, wouldn't she? To you, Jess?"

"I suppose so. If I had the money to buy."

"You will have, Jess. And then you'll be the biggest rancher on Wild Horse Creek, won't you? You'll head up the fight against Dollar. And when the split comes, you'll get the biggest share."

"Sure." Jess's voice was doubtful, for he still did not fully comprehend the sheriff's plan. "But what if Guy don't hang Arch?"

Freitag laughed nastily. "He will, Jess. He will. That's what I want you two for tonight."

VI

Immediately following the trial, Arch Dorrance and Sue drove out of Chimney Rock in a rented buggy. Sue was excessively pale in spite of the heat. The day had been an ordeal for her, yet one that she welcomed as penance for what she had done.

Unspeaking, they drove for nearly a full five miles. But at last Arch asked, his voice oddly humble: "What do we do now, Sue?"

She didn't look at him. Her voice was small, tight. "I guess that's for you to say, Arch. My things are packed."

Silence then, but at last he asked in a tortured voice: "Where did I let you down, Sue?"

Tears dimmed Sue's vision. Her eyes brimmed full and they ran across her cheeks to drop silently and unnoticed into her lap.

Arch's voice raised: "Where did I let you down? Where along the line did we stop being for each other and start pulling apart?"

She shook her head. "I don't know, Arch. Maybe it was too gradual to tell. But it wasn't your fault. It was me. I wanted too much . . . expected too much."

"But I should have given you what you wanted. That's what a husband's for."

She turned and met his glance. His eyes were filled with self-condemnation, but she could see something else there, too, something that would never leave. Hurt. Deep hurt because she had betrayed him for another man. He might eventually understand the things that had driven her to it. He might even forgive. But he would never forget. No matter how good the years were, this would always be between them.

She also knew that it was not for her to say what would happen now. That must be Arch's own decision. Bitterly, desperately

Sue wished she could go back in time a few short weeks, could live over this part of her life.

Arch said: "Sue, we could go away. Some place where neither of us is known."

"Whatever you say, Arch."

"Sure. We'll go away. We'll. . . ."

Sue put a hand on his arm, felt the muscles go rigid beneath it. She murmured: "Arch. Don't try to decide today. Be very sure that what you decide is really what you want. Don't think about me and don't worry about me."

His face contorted. His mouth twisted. His voice was a cry of pain. "Why did you do it? Sue, for heaven's sake, why?" He made a visible effort at regaining control of himself. His shoulders shook with his dry, silent weeping.

"I don't know, Arch. I don't know! I guess I'm just no good."

The silence again. Silence that lasted the remainder of the way home. He helped her out of the buggy, watched her as she walked to the house. Then he led the buggy horse away toward the barn.

Sue changed her clothes immediately and began to straighten and clean the house. She pushed herself, as though hard work could ease the tortured workings of her mind.

Arch stayed away until she called him in for supper. He ate in silence, replying with careful courtesy to her queries: "More meat, Arch?" or "There's plenty of everything, Arch. You're a big man. You need to eat."

And he tried. Tried to eat heartily as though nothing were wrong. After supper he packed his pipe and went outside again. Sue cleaned up the kitchen and washed the dishes. Then she sat down in the parlor to wait.

Arch came in at 10:00. His eyes were haunted, his mouth grim but stubbornly smiling. "Go to bed, Sue. I'll sleep here on the sofa."

Sue's breath went out of her in a slow sigh. She murmured: "All right, Arch."

She went silently into the bedroom and slipped out of her clothes. She lay down on the bed. She could not deny the empty feeling in her heart. She could not control the hot, scalding tears that flooded her eyes. Yet what had she expected? Quick forgiveness? Forgetting so soon? It was not to be that easy. Months would pass before Arch would kiss her again with any real feeling.

She blew out the lamp and pulled the single thin cover over her. The air was stifling, hot. Sue lay and stared at the ceiling with wide-open, unwinking eyes.

Arch sat very still on the sofa, listening to the familiar, intimate sounds of Sue undressing. He heard the *creak* of the bed as she lay down. He grimaced and buried his face in his hands.

More than anything else, he wanted to go in to her, to kiss her, to try and recapture the love that had once been between them.

It was fear that stopped him, that held him rooted here. Fear that, kissing her, he would be able to think of nothing but Rudy Coulter—fear that the old, wild, savage anger would rise in him again.

Two nights ago. It didn't seem possible that only two days had elapsed since he'd killed Rudy Coulter.

Arch had spent those two days and nights trying to forget the crazy, terrible rage that had possessed him upon entering the house that night and finding Sue in Rudy's arms. But he couldn't forget. He'd never forget. He'd go through his life from here on wondering when that killing fury would come upon him again.

Fear of it had kept him gentle with Sue today. But it had also kept him from going in to her tonight.

He knew he must stay away from Sue until the first intensity of his hatred for Rudy was gone. Else he'd be holding her in his arms some night, and he'd get to thinking of Rudy, and that insane murderous hatred would return.

Arch shuddered. He had been unable to restrain himself two nights ago. What if it happened again? What if he killed Sue?

He got up nervously and began to pace the floor. Back and forth. Back and forth. He strode to the door and went outside.

The night was like all nights were this summer. Hot and still. Hot enough to make a man sweat, just sitting.

He heard a commotion out in the yard. Horses moving about, nickering, biting, kicking. Hang it! He must have left the corral gate open. Thinking of his trouble, he must have left it open.

He went down off the low porch and walked through the dust across the yard. In the dim starlight, he could see the milling shapes of the horses. He turned to circle, to drive them back into the corral.

A voice nearby startled him, saying: "Arch?"

He whirled to face that voice. And heard the slightest of sounds behind him.

Something descended on his head, bringing a bitter, brackish taste to his mouth. The world reeled before his eyes and he could feel himself falling.

He heard low, cautious voices—and hit the ground. His last thought was: *Judas, Guy meant it after all. He's going to hang me. . . .*

When he wakened, he was slung, belly down, across the back of a horse. His hands and feet were tied together under the horse's belly. His belt was loosened and hooked over the saddle horn.

His head pounded savagely, and bright lights danced before his opened eyes. Dust swirled up from beneath the horse's hoofs, filling his mouth and nostrils, choking him. He coughed.

A voice said: "He's coming to, Karl."

"All right. We're almost there."

Arch found it hard to believe he was not dreaming. That first voice had been the voice of Jess Arnold, his neighbor. The answer had come from Karl Freitag, the sheriff.

Arch croaked: "Sheriff, what in the devil is going on? Take these ropes off me and let me down."

"Pretty soon, Arch. We're almost there."

"Almost where?"

"Where we're going. There's a big cottonwood right at the mouth of Dollar Creek. It's where Guy has always hung rustlers."

"Karl!" Arch choked on his own spittle. "What the devil are you going to do?"

Freitag failed to answer. But Jess cleared his throat uneasily.

Arch cried: "Jess, what's going on?"

He strained his head around, saw Jess Arnold's bulk atop the horse behind him. Behind Jess was another man, huge, broad. Jess didn't answer, so Arch said, growing desperate with a cold, helpless fear: "Is that you, Orvie?" He got no answer. He yelled: "Orvie! Jess! Karl! What the hell is this?"

Freitag said sharply: "Arch, you shut up, or I'll have to gag you."

Arch held his voice down with an effort. He said incredulously: "But you're all my friends. You were for me today in court. Why the about-face? *Why this?*"

"Just business, Arch. Now, you goin' to shut up, or do I have to clout you again?"

A chill began somewhere in Arch's spine and spread rapidly throughout his body until he was shivering violently. He clamped his jaws together to keep his teeth from chattering. He was helpless. There was no getting away. They were going to hang him, for no other reason than to revenge themselves for some unknown thing against Dollar.

The horses stopped and Freitag, Jess, and Orvie dismounted. They untied Arch from the saddle and hoisted him to the back of the horse, leaving his hands tied behind him.

Jess held the horse, Orvie held Arch, and Freitag tossed a rope over the cottonwood limb.

He mounted then, rode close, and fixed the loop over Arch's neck. Then he got down and hunted around while looking for a place to tie the rope.

Arch could see, in the faint starlight, that Jess Arnold was shaking almost as badly as Arch was himself. Orvie Gartrell stepped away, and his hand rose, holding a quirt.

Arch yelled—"Wait!"—in a loud and frantic voice. But the quirt came down, slashed the rump of Arch's horse. The horse made a sudden, frightened leap, and the rope tightened on Arch's neck. It bit deeply into his flesh. He flew out of the saddle, limp as a rag doll, and dangled, jerking and twitching at its end.

And he didn't even hear Freitag's voice, sounding as though the sheriff were all out of breath: "Come on. Let's get out of here."

VII

Diamondback Joe Ryecroft rolled out of his blankets in the cool of dawn. Lately he had taken to spending the night where darkness found him, and last night had been no exception.

Snake hunting had been exceptionally good all summer. Unbelievable as it seemed, the drought had driven even the rattlesnakes that needed little water away from their rocky dens, down the slopes, to water in the valley floor.

Joe built his fire, noticing this morning that there wasn't even any dew on the grass. It was that dry.

From the pack he carried on his back, but which now lay

beside the fire, Joe took a pan and a handful of dry beans and put them on to simmer. He spitted on a stick the rabbit he had shot last night and held it over the fire, turning it slowly until it began to steam and drip juice. The fire died down to red coals, and the rabbit began to brown.

Streaming sweat from the heat of the blaze, Joe moved away, ate his beans and his rabbit.

Then he gathered up his meager gear, packed it away, and slung the pack over his shoulder. And he was off to another day of snake hunting.

Yesterday he'd broken away long enough to go to town for the trial. So today he found himself in the valley's lower end, moving slowly up the course of Wild Horse Creek.

He killed a snake two miles below the place where Dollar Creek joined Wild Horse Creek, another no more than 300 yards from that place.

Looking up from cutting the rattles off this one, he saw the body, hanging from the limb of the cottonwood, turning ever so slowly.

He didn't start. He made no sudden move. But his eyes widened and his breath came sighing quickly out from between his thinned, cracked lips.

He said softly to himself: "Goddlemighty. Guy meant it after all."

He walked over and looked up at Arch's body. It wasn't a pretty sight. It had the effect of making Diamondback Joe violently angry. Because this was wrong—all wrong.

Guy should have showed better sense than this. Guy should have known that this would only trigger off the worst trouble the valley had ever seen. Ute trouble would seem like nothing beside it. Joe wondered, suddenly, if anyone else knew about this.

Probably not. Else the body would have been cut down.

So Joe swung around and headed at a fast walk toward town. This much did Joe want to do—notify the sheriff first, so that perhaps the trouble might be controlled or averted. For Joe knew if he reported this to the first Wild Horse Creek rancher he saw, it would not be noon before a mob of well-armed ranchers would be thundering north toward Dollar.

Joe hurried along at a fast, shuffling walk. A mile out of town a snake rattled at him, and Joe didn't even take time to kill it. Even so, it was almost noon when he came into town.

He went at once to the adobe jail building. Karl Freitag sat behind his desk, his feet propped upon it. He looked up as Joe entered, more alert than usual, even a little nervous, it seemed to Joe.

Joe said: "Well, Sheriff, Guy went an' done it." He was puzzled at the quick darkening of Freitag's face, at the sudden hostility in the sheriff's eyes.

But Freitag recovered himself quickly, asking: "Done what, Joe?"

"Hung Arch," said Joe. "He's danglin' from that old cottonwood at the forks where Dollar has always hung their rustlers."

Freitag got to his feet, giving an impression of extreme weariness. "All right, Joe. I'll get some men together and we'll go cut him down. How do you know it was Guy that did it? You find tracks?" He seemed anxious, saying this.

Joe said: "Why, Sheriff, I didn't think to look for tracks. But it must've been Guy. Nobody else would do somethin' like that to Arch."

"Guess not."

Freitag went out into the blazing heat and walked toward town and Reilly's saloon. Joe Ryecroft turned his face away from town and resumed his slow, methodical plodding course upcountry. Twenty minutes after leaving town, he saw Freitag riding along the road at a fast trot, with three men and a buckboard behind him.

At dawn, Knox Coulter saddled a horse and rode downcountry. In his belt was stuffed the Colt .44 that he had taken away from Sue Dorrance a couple of days before. He intended to return it today and this would give him an opportunity to talk to Arch.

Knox still hoped to avert the trouble that he knew Guy would try to start. And since Arch would now be the recognized leader of the Wild Horse Creek bunch, he was the logical one to talk to about it. If Arch could be persuaded to counsel patience and thus keep the smaller ranchers in line, then perhaps Knox would have some chance of talking Guy out of starting anything.

Dollar ranch house lay almost seven miles from the forks where Dollar Creek and Wild Horse Creek joined. So it was nearly sunup when Knox reached the Dorrance place.

He saw Arch's body at once, saw it and knew a terrible, sinking sickness in his mind. So Guy had done it after all? Damn him! *Damn him!*

Hadn't he seen what this would do to the country? Was he so intent on his petty, personal vengeance that he didn't care? Or was this hanging only Guy's way of opening the ball, so that war in the valley would become inevitable, this giving him his opportunity to seize Wild Horse Ridge?

Knox stared at the swinging body a moment more. Humanity demanded that he cut Arch down. It was indecent to leave him here.

Knox moved toward him, fighting his horse because the animal was thoroughly terrified at the sight of Arch and entirely unmanageable.

Then Knox saw the wisp of smoke rising over there beyond the creek, the smoke from Diamondback Joe's campfire. And, looking back toward Dollar, he saw young Dave Coulter coming along the road, following Knox's own tracks.

So Knox whirled his horse, dug in his spurs, and let the relieved animal run along the road that led back toward Dollar.

He intercepted Dave before the boy could see Arch's swinging body and caught at his bridle reins. "Where you going, kid?"

Dave looked sheepish, a little scared. "Following you."

"Well, we're going back."

Knox tried to conceal his worry from the boy, tried to make his grin genuine. He knew he had failed when Dave said: "What's the matter, Knox? You look like you'd seen a ghost."

Knox was wondering how long it would be before Arch's body was discovered. And how long after that it would be before a mob of angry Wild Horse Creek ranchers descended on Dollar. Half a day, at most, he guessed. He said: "Nothing's the matter, Dave. Now let's go back."

The sun beat hotly against their backs as they rode. Dust rose in a cloud behind them. And anger began to build in Knox's mind. Which of the crew members had helped Guy last night? Red? Frank Roberts? Dutch Holcomb? Guy would have had to pick his crew carefully, choosing only those who would have a stomach for such a chore, and who would keep still about it afterward. Knox crossed Red Daly off the list. Red would refuse, he knew. Frank Roberts was different. And so was Dutch. Both of them were capable of a hanging. And neither would talk about it afterward.

So there was no use in Knox trying to get the story out of them. He'd have to go straight to the old man.

He and Dave rode in at a lope. Already the crew had scattered, taking up their day's work. Knox handed the reins of his horse to Dave with the curt words: "Put him up. I've got to talk to Guy."

And strode away purposefully into the house.

56

★ ★ ★ ★ ★

Dave was ten. That wasn't very old, he guessed, but it was old enough to sense when something was terribly wrong.

He hesitated but an instant, holding the reins of Knox's horse. Then defiantly he dismounted and tied both horses to the branch of a cottonwood tree. Trotting silently, he went around the side of the house and came up under the open window of Dollar's office.

He heard Knox's voice, raised and angry: "Guy, that was a lousy, sneaky thing to do! Who helped you? Dutch Holcomb? Frank Roberts?"

"Helped me do what? Blame you, Knox, don't use that tone of voice on me!"

"And don't you sit there and lie to me, either! Arch Dorrance is hanging from that cottonwood down at the forks!"

Both of them were shouting now. Shouting and raging, crazy mad. Dave's eyes were wide with fright. He was sweating and shivering at the same time. He wanted, more than anything else, to run, to hide, to pretend that this wasn't happening.

But it was happening. And there was no escape. Horror beat through the boy's mind. Arch Dorrance hanging from the cottonwood down at the forks—Knox accusing his father of doing that!

Guy's voice became dangerously soft. "So you think I would hang Arch in the night and lie about it afterward?"

"Didn't you?" Knox's voice had not softened. He was still shouting. In his voice was outrage, shock, raw anger. "You know what will happen now, don't you? As soon as the Wild Horse Creek bunch finds him, they'll be riding for Dollar. Fifteen or twenty of them. Gunning for you, and me, and whoever else gets in their way."

Dave had never heard Guy's voice the way it was then. It wasn't loud, but it was venomous, dangerous. It said: "Get out

57

of here, Knox, before I kill you. Get out!"

Dave edged upward, peeked over the window sill. Guy stood with his back to the window, so the boy could not see the expression on his face. But he could see Knox's face. It was white with rage. Knox's hands were shaking. Knox stormed: "Greed! Greed! More grass, more water! Don't you ever think of anything else? I'm beginning to think the country's right about you, right about Dollar. You're like Rudy, you take what you want, whether it's a man's grass or his wife."

Guy, suddenly shaking with his fury, yanked open the drawer of his desk. His hand came up with an old Colt .45.

And Dave, wild with fear, putting forth an effort he had not thought possible, raised himself and scrambled through the window. The gun was coming up, slowed because Guy took an instant to look behind him. Knox stood, frozen, unbelieving of what he saw.

Dave tumbled through the window and threw himself at Guy's legs, clutching with both arms. Guy staggered, fell heavily to the floor.

Dave screamed: "Knox, get out! Get out before he kills you!"

And Knox did. Knox must have seen that there was no halting this now. It had gone too far. Rage had maddened Guy, had made him uncaring of what happened next. He would have fired that gun had not Dave dived at his legs and upset him.

So Knox went out. Dave released his father's legs and came to his feet, waiting for the savage beating he was likely to get, waiting for the terrible, bitter words that Guy would use on him like a whip.

He waited, and he waited, and at last dared to raise his eyes to Guy's face.

It was twisted with pain. Guy's eyes were brimming with unshed tears. And he was still shaking, but no longer from rage. From reaction, from the letdown, but not from rage.

Dave's voice was scarcely audible: "I'm sorry, Pa. I'm sorry."

"Sorry? *Sorry,* boy? Oh my Lord!"—and he collapsed into the chair and buried his face in his hands.

Outside, faintly, Dave heard the rapid drum of hoofs as Knox rode away. Sickness came to Dave's stomach, and his face turned gray. He jumped to his feet, ran to the window, and, hanging weakly on the sill, retched until his stomach was empty.

Then, sweating, he ran from the room, ran to his own small room, and flung himself face downward on the bed. And cried until he could cry no more.

Knox's face was flushed with rage as he threw himself upon his horse and thundered down the lane and away from Dollar. He was deeply shocked at the realization that his own father had been on the verge of killing him.

Why? *Why?* Had lust for power and for revenge against Arch reached the proportions of madness in Guy? Knox shook his head slowly. That seemed the only answer.

For a full two miles, Knox galloped his horse hard. Then, suddenly realizing that the animal was soaked with sweat and winding fast, Knox pulled him to a walk.

It was yet early in the day. Perhaps no later than 8:00. Something drew Knox onward, down the road toward Wild Horse Creek, although he knew it might be extremely dangerous for him to be seen there.

But he had no place else to go. The doors at Dollar were now closed to him since Guy had driven him out. Chimney Rock would be too dangerous for anyone from Dollar in broad daylight. Yet he kept on riding, not quite knowing why.

He came at last to the forks and was mildly surprised to see Arch's body still hanging there. He thought again of cutting Arch down, but, instead, he rode around the body, his eyes on the ground.

He picked out four separate sets of tracks. Since Arch would have been riding one horse, that meant that three men had brought him here and hanged him.

Arch's body, slowly turning above him gave him a cold, uneasy feeling. He looked up at the man who had once been his friend, who was now dead because he had been caught up in a vicious set of circumstances that were not of his making at all. One of Arch's hands hung limply open, the other was clenched into a fist. A fly *buzzed* around Arch's head. Knox scowled. "Judas! I ought to cut him down."

He dismounted, fished out his pocket knife, and walked toward the cottonwood where the rope was tied.

Arch's body drew his glance again, and that clenched fist. Why would Arch die with his fist clenched? Had he been shaking it at them as he died, or . . . or was something in his hand?

Controlling his stomach with difficulty, Knox walked over, reached up, and pried open Arch's fingers. A small bit of metal fell into his hand. He turned away from Arch and stared down at it.

It was a brass name plate. One of the many Orvie Gartrell had sent east for a couple of years ago. It read:

Property of Chimney Rock Stables.
Chimney Rock, Colo.

Orvie had kept losing saddles. So he'd hit upon the idea of putting these tags on each of his livery stable saddles. In fact, he had put the tags on almost everything he owned.

Arch's having one in his hand didn't mean much. Except that Knox may have been dead wrong in accusing Guy of the hanging. Guy would hardly hire a livery stable horse from Orvie for the job. It wouldn't make sense.

Another question began to puzzle Knox, that being why Arch had the tag in his hand anyway. *Why* would he work the tag loose and hold it clutched so tightly?

Well, one thing was fairly sure. Knox had made a fool of himself, accusing Guy this morning. No wonder his father had been mad. And if Guy had had nothing to do with Arch's death, as now appeared possible, Knox knew he'd be foolish to touch the body.

So he mounted up and rode downcountry toward town, only, instead of taking the valley road, he climbed his horse up into the cedars and stayed within their thick and fragrant concealment.

VIII

At 9:00 that morning, Jess Arnold rode into the yard at Dorrance's place and swung ponderously down from his saddle.

Smoke curled up from the stone chimney. Jess waddled over to the back door and knocked. The door opened immediately, and Jess could tell from this that Sue had been waiting just behind it, probably having seen him ride in.

Her smile was wan and without warmth. "Good morning, Mister Arnold."

"Arch t'home?" Jess made his voice casual, expectant.

Sue shook her head.

"You know where he is, ma'am? I'd like to see him." He wondered if this were sounding right and he couldn't tell. Because it took some acting to ask a man's wife where her husband was when you knew all the time he was hanging from a cottonwood limb not three miles away.

"I'm sorry, I don't know, Mister Arnold. He . . ."—she hesitated, then went on, bravely meeting his glance—"he hasn't been home all night."

Jess clucked sympathetically and looked away with every appearance of embarrassment. "Well, if you see him, just tell him I was here. I was kind of figurin'. . . ." It was Jess's turn to hesitate.

61

Sue asked: "Figuring what, Mister Arnold?"

"Well." He coughed. "I was figurin' mebbe you folks'd be leavin' now, on account of . . . well, the trouble. I live next to you and I calc'lated, was you goin' to sell, why I'd try to buy."

Sue made a weak smile. "That's very kind of you. I'll tell Arch when he comes back."

"Thanks, ma'am."

Sue closed the door and Jess turned away. He was smiling, he realized, with a certain triumph. He had planted the seed in Sue's mind now. When the news of Arch's death reached her, she'd remember Jess's offer, and would probably send him word that she was ready to sell.

Jess rode away from Arch's place and took the road toward town. He wondered if Arch's body had been discovered yet. He passed Joe Ryecroft and noticed that Joe was shuffling rather purposefully toward town. But Joe was a couple of hundred yards off the road, so Jess satisfied himself with a wave at the little man, a wave that Joe did not return.

Jess pushed his horse a little harder than usual, and so came into Chimney Rock a little before noon. He went at once to Reilly's saloon.

Orvie Gartrell was standing at the end of the bar, a bottle and glass before him. Orvie was already a little drunk. He stared at Jess owlishly, paled, and looked away quickly, pouring himself another drink and downing it at a gulp. Orvie looked as though he had not slept last night.

And Jess could understand that. He hadn't slept himself. Every time he'd closed his eyes, he'd seen Arch's body as it yanked free of the saddle and hung, swaying and jerking at the end of the rope.

He found himself a place at the bar and ordered a bottle and glass. He drank two as quickly as he could pour and toss them down. Then he poured the third and stood staring at it, while the warmth of the first two smoldered in his stomach. He began to sweat, and pulled a dirty bandanna from his pocket and wiped his face.

The saloon slowly emptied as the townsmen went home for dinner one by one. And at last all that remained were Jess, Orvie, and the bartender, Reilly, who said, grinning: "You boys are hitting it kind of heavy today, ain't you? What you trying to forget?"

Orvie, down at the end of the bar, snarled savagely: "Shut your damned mouth, Reilly."

Jess drank another, poured another. And looked at that one for a while.

There was nothing for either him or Orvie to do but wait. There'd be action sometime today, though. Arch's body would be found and Freitag would head out of town with a posse.

Almost as though his thinking had brought the desired result, Karl Freitag chose that moment to shoulder into the saloon. He yelled: "Arch Dorrance's been hung! I want some help to go get his body, and after that I want a posse to go after Guy Coulter." He looked at Orvie Gartrell and his lips curled with contempt. He said harshly: "You sober enough to ride, Orvie?"

"I reckon I am." Orvie's tone was surly.

Freitag turned to Jess. "How about you?"

"Sure, Sheriff."

"All right then. Orvie, you go down to the livery stable and hitch up a buckboard. The county'll pay you for the use of it. Jess, you go out and round up two, three more men. Meet me back here quick as you can."

Jess heaved his bulk away from the bar, downed the drink before him, and walked unsteadily to the door. Because it was hot, he mounted his horse and rode as far as Hazeltree's. He spotted old Will Hazeltree inside the store, saw his son Josh with him.

He called in the door from the street, "Will! Sheriff wants a couple of men. You come?"

Will and the boy came to the door.

Will asked: "What's up?"

"Arch's been hung."

Will turned to Josh. "Watch the store. I'll go."

"Aw, Dad. Let me go."

"Won't be pretty," said Hazeltree. "Won't be pretty at all. Nothin' for a boy to see. You watch the store."

Jess said: "Sheriff's waitin' at Reilly's."

"All right. Be there quick as I can saddle up."

Hazeltree went around to the back of the store.

Jess picked up another man off the street, a neighbor of his named Ray Sullivan, who was just riding in off the Wild Horse Creek road. Together they headed for Reilly's.

Jess had another drink and Ray had a beer, and by that time they heard Orvie drive up outside with the buckboard. Freitag stuck his head inside the door and shouted—"Come on, you two!"—and Jess and Ray went out.

Four of them riding, and Orvie driving the buckboard, in the back of which was a canvas tarpaulin to wrap Arch's body in.

They pressed along pretty hard, considering the day's heat, not talking at all, except for Hazeltree, who occasionally said: "By George, I wouldn't have thought it of Guy. Reckoned he had better sense."

And except for Ray Sullivan, who would invariably reply to that: "Well, he'll be sorry. I guess he'll be plenty sorry he did."

When they reached the forks where Arch's body hung, Freitag said: "Orvie, drive the buckboard under him. I'll stand in the bed and cut him loose. Jess, you git up here and ease him down."

Orvie fought the frightened horses into place, so that the buckboard was almost under Arch's body. Jess sat still on his horse, pale and filled with nausea. Freitag looked at him with unconcealed contempt, then said: "All right, Hazeltree. You're used to dead bodies. You git up here then."

Hazeltree did, and Freitag cut the rope. Arch's body *thumped* into the back of the buckboard, and Hazeltree dragged the canvas over it.

Freitag said: "All right. You go back with Orvie, Will. Jess and Ray and me will ride Wild Horse Creek till we get up a posse."

Jess was beginning to get the pitch now. Freitag would get up a posse fifteen or twenty strong and made up entirely of the Wild Horse Creek bunch. He'd ride to Dollar and demand Guy's surrender.

Jess said: "Karl, I guess you know that Guy will never give up."

And Freitag laughed harshly. "Who cares? If he won't give up, we'll take him if we have to kill every hand on Dollar to do it."

Jess could not repress a slight shudder, and he suddenly wondered if he would not have been smarter last night to tell Freitag to go to hell. He had an uneasy hunch that whatever the penalty was for the crime he had committed back in Kansas, it would be lighter than what was coming to him here.

IX

Bruce Adams was the first of the Wild Horse Creek ranchers that Jess called upon. He found Bruce at the upper end of his hay field, fixing fence. Not that there was anything in the hay field to fence this year, but Bruce was the kind that hated to be idle.

Jess said: "Sheriff's getting up a posse to go after Guy Coulter. Guy hung Arch Dorrance from the cottonwood at the forks last night."

Bruce's face immediately darkened.

Jess said: "Get your horse and tell your wife you're going."

Bruce's face remained angry, but his eyes took on a certain caution. He said: "You know Dollar will fight. How many men's Freitag going to take?"

"All he can get." Jess turned his horse. "Fifteen or twenty, maybe. We'll meet at the forks."

He rode away before Bruce could say anything more. Looking back, he saw Bruce gathering up his tools preparatory to heading for the house. He noticed the hesitation in Bruce, but he dismissed it from his mind.

Next, he rode in at Les Borden's. It was a different story here. Borden was a dark, squat man with a graying beard and a wild kind of light in his eyes. When Jess told his news, Borden's eyes narrowed, and his lips set in a firm, straight line. "Wait till I get my rifle. By Judas, it's time we taught that Dollar bunch a thing or two."

Jess rode out, calling back: "Meet at the forks!"

At Borden's gate, up on the road, Jess could hear Borden's wife scolding him in her shrill voice.

Jess called at four more places. Of the four, only one man flatly refused to go. Two of them, however, were cautious and a little reluctant, as Bruce Adams had been.

Finished, Jess turned and rode back toward the forks. He arrived in late afternoon, and there were already a dozen men at the meeting place, among them Bruce Adams, Les Borden, Freitag, and Ray Sullivan.

They were gathered under the cottonwood from which Arch Dorrance had been hung, taking advantage of the shade. The sun beat down today upon an airless, dusty land, causing shimmering distortion of everything a man looked at.

All of the men here were sweaty, hot, and angry. Freitag said as Jess rode up: "This is a lawful thing I'm asking you all to do. I'll deputize every one of you and swear you in. I want Guy

Coulter for the murder of Arch Dorrance, and I want the men that helped him."

Bruce Adams cleared his throat. His voice was grave, and perhaps a little reluctant. "Dollar's going to fight, Karl. You think it's wise to go about it this way?"

Freitag snorted contemptuously. "You know a better way, Bruce? Hang it, Dollar's been twenty years in this country, ridin' roughshod over everything and everybody that stood in its way. They've served notice on you by killin' Arch that you'd better not dare even to defend your wives and homes. You think we ought to skirt around it? I say let's ride, and, if Dollar wants a fight, we'll give 'em a fight they'll remember a long while."

There was a chorus of approving cheers at this from the hot-headed members of the group, Les Borden among them. But Bruce Adams's jaw set stubbornly. Jess could see this group already breaking up into two factions, one of them counseling patience, or at least careful planning, the other immediate, violent action.

Jess couldn't have said which side he favored. He knew that Freitag's plan was to wipe out the Coulters — Guy and Knox and probably little Dave, too. For only by so doing would Dollar be vacated and free for the taking.

Jess was also beginning to feel a tiny, nagging suspicion that Orvie and himself were but tools in Freitag's hands, to be discarded or destroyed when their usefulness was done.

Freitag looked at him hard, and said: "Jess, speak up. Let's hear where you stand on this. You're the biggest of the Wild Horse bunch. Speak your piece."

Jess cleared his throat. The whiskey he had drunk this morning had left only a dull ache in his head. Its stimulation was entirely gone. He looked at Freitag, looked around at the faces of his neighbors. He tried to sound angry, but it didn't quite come off. "I say let's go get Guy. If his help wants to butt in, why we'll discourage 'em. But the court cleared Arch yesterday, and if we let Guy get away with hanging him, how long do you think we'll have our places on Wild Horse Creek, or our grass up on the ridge? Everybody knows Guy wants that."

Adams said: "Maybe Guy just wants us to jump Dollar. Maybe that's why he hung Arch last night. Maybe he's forted up at Dollar, just hoping we'll come barging in."

There was an agreeing chorus to this. Freitag's color rose, and his eyes narrowed. He started to speak angrily, but clamped his jaws shut before he had said a word. He whirled, put his back to the bunch of them, and strode away. He whirled again and came back. He said: "Damn it, I'm sheriff of this county. The rest of you are residents of the same county. By the Lord Harry, I can deputize you whether you like it or not. And once I do that, you'll do what you're told!"

There was a stubborn set to Adams's jaw, an odd light in his eyes. He said softly: "Try deputizing me against my will, Karl. Try it."

That seemed to calm Freitag instantly. He became conciliatory, almost pleading. "Listen, boys. We'll wait till night if it'll make you feel any better. We'll wait until night. But we've got to take Guy. Hell, Arch was a nice guy. He didn't do anything wrong. The court said what he did wasn't wrong." He looked at Adams, whose wife was young and pretty. "Bruce, what would you do if you came home and . . . ?"

Bruce said dangerously: "Shut up, Karl!"

"No offense meant. It wouldn't happen to you. But supposing it did?"

Adams asked: "How do you propose to do this? You want Guy and whoever helped him hang Arch. But I know a lot of those boys up at Dollar, and I like them. I like Knox, and I'd hate to see little Dave get hurt. It won't do to just barge in there and start shooting."

Freitag's voice grew plaintive. "Who said I planned it that way?"

Ray Sullivan said: "You did, Sheriff."

"Well, I didn't mean it. I was mad when we found Arch. He was a friend of mine. Maybe I spoke a little hasty. But who wouldn't?"

Now, three more men joined the group, these being from the farthermost ranches away up at the head of Wild Horse Creek.

Freitag said, as though the thing were settled: "We'll wait till night. That way we can get Guy without kicking up a fuss."

And Adams subsided grumbling.

Freitag swore them in, and checked their rifles and revolvers. He watched them scatter out, some of them lying down to sleep, others gathering in small groups to talk. Jess Arnold wandered off by himself at a sign from the sheriff, and shortly thereafter Freitag joined him. "Ride into town and get Orvie," he said.

"What for? We got enough men."

Freitag looked at him pityingly. "Enough men, but not the right kind. You fool, don't you understand anything? It's going to be up to you and Orvie and me to see that Guy don't get a chance to give up peacefully tonight. I want him and Knox both to get it."

Jess supposed he should take Freitag's word that this was possible, this steal of Dollar. He said doubtfully: "Well, all right. But what good's it going to do? You can't just take a place because the owners get killed."

Freitag laughed. "That's where you're wrong. Dollar ain't an owned ranch except for the hundred and sixty acres the buildings sit on. All the rest, the valley and Dry Ridge, Dollar holds by the priority of previous usage . . . in other words force. Anyone that can take Dollar owns it. And I m going to take Dollar. That is, you and me and Orvie are. Now go on into town and get Orvie."

Jess shrugged. "All right." He walked back to the cottonwood, got his horse, and mounted. He rode out along the road toward town. His face, with its rolls of fat, was bland and without expression.

His tiny, close-set black eyes looked out on the blazing land with crafty coldness. His uneasy feeling about Freitag was gone now. He had at last recognized that Freitag had no intention of splitting Dollar with him and Orvie. It wasn't death that Freitag planned for them. Freitag meant to expose them both, Jess Arnold on that old Kansas charge, Orvie for murdering the whiskey drummer who was buried in his back yard.

When he did, who would believe Orvie's and Jess's protestations, or their charge that they had helped Freitag hang Arch? No one. No one at all. Therefore, it was only good sense that Jess protect himself. First, he'd go to Freitag's office and get that dodger. And sometime tonight, in the thick of the battle at Dollar, Freitag was going to stop a bullet—from behind.

Jess began to chuckle softly, deeply, away down inside his fat body.

X

From the cedars above the road, Knox Coulter saw the group headed by Sheriff Freitag and followed by Orvie's buckboard ride up the road, and knew from this that Arch's body had at last been discovered.

For an instant, he debated riding down there, intercepting Freitag and telling him of the livery stable tag he had found in Arch's hand. He realized almost at once, however, that the sheriff would not believe him. Not only that, but he'd probably be taken into custody on suspicion of having a hand in Arch's death.

Riding on, he took the metal tag out of his pocket and looked at it thoughtfully. In Knox's mind, at least, the thing cleared

Guy. And if it cleared Guy, it implicated someone else. But who? Who in the devil would want to hang Arch, unless it was a deliberate attempt to ruin Guy and Dollar?

An odd sense of urgency began to overcome Knox, and he gigged his horse into a fast trot. He circled town, coming up toward it along the river bottom that was lined with willows and therefore offered some concealment. He left his horse tied to one of the willows and approached the town on foot.

Orvie's livery barn was, save for two abandoned buildings, the closest building in town to the river. Knox reached its rear door, he believed, unobserved, and went inside.

It was a huge building, with a hayloft overhead. The interior was made up of two long alleys, a double row of stalls down the middle, and stalls along each wall. The tack room and Orvie's office were up front.

Buggies and buckboards were parked in one of the alleys, leaving the other clear. There were perhaps a dozen horses in the stable, stamping and switching their tails at flies.

Knox moved quickly to the front of the building and stepped into the tack room.

Orvie was a tidy man. Bridles and harness hung neatly from pegs driven into the wall. Saddles hung from ropes suspended from the rafters, making it easy for Knox to locate those with missing tags.

There were three of these. Knox looked at them all carefully. Two of the saddles had apparently been without tags for some time, since the leather under the place the tags had been was weathered and dusty. The third, however, was different. The place the tag had been was clearly noticeable because the leather there had a new appearance. And Knox noticed something else. Crudely scratched on the leather of the cantle were the letters *FRI.*

Puzzling maybe, for an instant. But when you put things

together, it became less puzzling. The tag in Arch's hand cleared Guy. It also proved that one of Orvie's saddles had been on the horse that carried Arch to his hanging.

The three letters must be the first three letters of someone's name, put there by Arch in a last minute, desperate attempt to name his killer.

Knox heard a voice out in front of the stable, heard the office door slam. Orvie's little brother Pete, apparently watching the stable while Orvie was gone, said: "Yes, sir. Any particular kind of horse?"

Knox knew the boy had a customer, and would soon be coming into the tack room for a saddle. He grabbed the saddle he had been looking at, unhooked it, and went to the door. The customer, who was Sam DeAndrea, had his back to the stable, lighting a cigar. Pete Gartrell was somewhere in the rear of the stable.

Knox ducked out of the tack room into the alley that held all the buggies and buckboards. He crouched down behind one of these until Pete had led the horse up front, saddled him, and turned him over to Sam.

After that, Pete went back into the office and Sam DeAndrea rode away.

Knox released a long, slow breath. He got up and went to the rear door, still carrying the saddle. When he got back there, he concealed it beneath a pile of old, worn-out buggy tops.

His mind, as he stepped outside, was going over the people of the town, searching for one whose name began with the letters F-R-I.

He passed over Freitag, since the first three letters of his name were F-R-E. He thought of old Jimmy Frye, discarded him, too. Jimmy wouldn't harm anything.

The trouble was, Knox didn't know everybody in Chimney

Rock by name. And then he thought of Nell. Nell would know everyone.

Walking fast, but staying in the alley and cutting through vacant lots, Knox approached the DeAndrea house at the rear door.

He knocked, briefly wondering if anyone had seen him, and, if so, what they would do about it. Freitag was out of town, and, with him gone, it was unlikely anyone would try to cause Knox trouble.

Nell called from inside the house: "Who is it?"

Knox didn't want to shout his name, so he stepped inside. Once in the kitchen he said: "It's Knox."

She came into the kitchen after a few moments and it was at once apparent that she had been dressing to go out. She said breathlessly: "I was getting ready to go up to Dorrance's place. Sue's going to need someone."

"You've heard then."

"Yes." Her eyes were troubled.

Knox asked: "No questions?"

"Oh, Knox, of course not." She came over and laid a hand on his arm, a firm, confident hand.

He grinned wryly. "I'll bet half the people in this town aren't so sure I didn't have anything to do with it."

She stood close to him, smelling sweet and fresh. Knox put his arms around her waist. She asked: "Have you left Dollar?"

He nodded. "I jumped Guy about Arch early this morning. I guess maybe I was the first to find Arch. Guy hit the ceiling. We had quite a fight. I believe he'd have shot me if Dave hadn't butted in."

"Why did he do it, Knox? Why?"

"That's the funny part of it. I don't think he did do it."

"What are you talking about?"

He held out the tag and she took it from him. He said: "That was clutched in Arch's hand. And he used it to scratch three letters on the cantle of the saddle before he died. They were F-R-I. You know anyone with a name beginning like that?"

Nell's lovely eyes were puzzled. "You mean Arch was taken to the place and was hanged on a livery stable horse?"

"The saddle anyway. Nell, would Guy hire a horse and saddle from Orvie to go hang Arch? Heck no, he wouldn't. There's plenty of horses and saddles at Dollar."

"How did you find out about the letters scratched on the saddle?"

He grinned. "Snooping in Orvie's livery barn. I've got the saddle hidden."

Nell frowned. She said: "Well, there's Jimmy Frye."

"I thought of him."

"And there's Freitag."

"Yeah. But the first three letters of his name are F-R-E."

Nell's face brightened. "Maybe Arch didn't get time to finish the E."

But Knox shook his head. "Freitag's sheriff. He was sticking up for Arch in the jail the other night. He wouldn't even have arrested him if Guy hadn't insisted on it."

Nell pulled herself away and walked to the window. When she turned back to him, her face was troubled, and a little pale. She said: "It was hot last night, Knox. Before I went to bed, I went for a little walk. About ten, I saw three men ride out of town. One was Orvie Gartrell, another was Sheriff Freitag. I'm not real sure of the third. But it looked like Jess Arnold."

Knox started to speak, but she silenced him.

"Wait, Knox. Perhaps I shouldn't have told you. What you have isn't evidence. It's not enough to go on."

"It's more than they've got on Guy," he muttered bitterly.

Nell murmured: "Just promise me you'll not do anything hasty because of what I've told you. I don't think I'm wrong, but I could be."

Knox felt again that peculiar sense of urgency, and he realized that soon, possibly even now, Freitag would be moving against Dollar. He had one more thought, and he asked: "How many horses did they have, Nell? Three or four?"

Nell's lips parted slightly. Her eyes were wide, her voice the merest whisper. "They had four, Knox. Orvie was leading one."

Knox grabbed her, gave her a quick, excited hug. "Nell, that's it, then! That's it. I don't know why they did it, but I know they did."

Her arms went around him with sudden strength, and her lips murmured: "Be careful, Knox. Oh, be careful, won't you?"

He grinned down at her. "Sure. Sure I will." He kissed her, intending that this be quick, but it didn't turn out that way. The touch of her lips seemed to set him on fire, and, when he drew away, he was breathless. He said: "Nell, I'll see you when I get back. You and me have got something to talk about."

And he went quickly out the door.

XI

Knox shortened his trip slightly by cutting across the cedar benches, and at the same time kept himself out of sight of the riders in the bottom. He saw them moving up the valley of Dollar Creek at sundown. By their leisurely pace, he judged that they were timing themselves so as to arrive after darkness had fallen.

It was dusk when Knox himself arrived at Dollar. He rode in, put his horse in the corral, and approached the house.

Convinced now that Guy had not hanged Arch, he blamed himself bitterly for his accusations of this morning. No wonder Guy had been enraged. He'd been accused and convicted by his own son without even a chance to deny the charge.

Usually at this time of evening, Dollar's crew lounged in the open around cook shack and bunkhouse, smoking, talking. Tonight the yard was entirely bare. No smoke rose from the chimney on the cookhouse roof.

Red Daly hailed him from the loft of the barn, and Knox saw that Red had a rifle in his hand. "Come back for the fireworks, kid?"

Knox grinned and stepped into the house. Old Guy stood in the middle of the kitchen floor. His eyes were frosty and hard, his mouth grim and unsmiling.

Guy said: "Get the devil out of here."

Young Dave stood behind Guy, his face tortured and twisted with his divided loyalties. He tried to look hard at Knox, but something pleading crept into his glance. Like all kids, Knox guessed, Dave was intensely disturbed by family disunity.

Knox said stiffly: "I was wrong. I know you didn't have anything to do with Arch's hanging. But you oughtn't to blame me for believing what all the rest of the country believes. You threatened to do it."

Guy's glance didn't waver. Knox couldn't tell if he was softening or not. Knox held out the metal tag. Guy hesitated for an instant, then asked: "What the devil's that?"

"I found it in Arch's hand after I left here this morning. I went to town and snooped around in Orvie's stable. I found the saddle it came off of. Arch scratched three letters on the cantle of the saddle before he died . . . F-R-I."

Guy frowned.

Knox went on: "Nell thought maybe Arch was trying to print Freitag, and didn't get time to finish the E. She said she saw Freitag ride out of town last night about ten with Orvie and Jess Arnold. They were leading a horse."

"Why the devil would Freitag want to hang Arch?"

"Because the whole country would think you did it. Freitag's on his way up Dollar Creek right now with about fifteen men.

Has Freitag got reason to hate you for anything?"

Guy shrugged. "Don't know why he should. I've always supported him at election time."

"Maybe he wants Dollar."

"You're loco! He'd have to kill all three of us to get it."

"Two of us. You and me. Dave couldn't hold it, and Freitag would know that."

Guy began to grin, a grin that wasn't pleasant. "Freitag's got a surprise comin' to him. The crew's armed with rifles and they're hid out all over the place. Have been all day."

Knox muttered: "That's one way out, but it isn't the right way, and you know it. There's only three men in that posse that know what's going on. The rest really think you killed Arch."

"So what?"

"They're good men. I'd hate to see any of them hurt. And if you fight, where will it get you? You'd be resisting the law. Any killing, and you'll eventually have to answer for it in court."

Guy thought about that for a moment, his face souring visibly. When he spoke, his voice held biting sarcasm. "I suppose you want me to surrender to Freitag. You think I'd ever reach town if I did?"

Knox shook his head slowly. In this moment he came out of the state where he was his father's son, dependent to some degree on his father for strength, and became entirely his own man, independent and decisive in his own right. He said: "I want you to run."

For an instant Guy stared at him uncomprehendingly. "*Run?* Kid, are you plumb loco?"

"You know a better way? You want to stay here and fight it out with that posse? I'm telling you, there're a lot of good men in that bunch. And there're a lot of good men hid out in the yard. Some of them are going to die if you make them fight."

Guy made his own fight, standing there, his fight between

pride and sense. Pride was telling him, as Knox could see, that this was Dollar, this was home, and he had a right to defend it. He had done nothing wrong.

Then sense took hold of him, and that was visible, too. He had made a fool of himself with those threats. Maybe somewhere in the recesses of his mind he'd meant to carry out his threats. But the sense went further. It told him that he'd been using Rudy's killing as a wedge, a mere excuse to make his steal of Wild Horse Ridge.

Knox saw the change come over Guy, saw the pride go out of him, and wished he had let his father alone. The pride went out, and there was nothing much left. Knox came to the bitter, instant realization that much of his father's character was built on pride, for the pride contained the arrogance, and the arrogance gave him his power. Now the power was gone, and Guy was only an aging man with gray, thinning hair and his Coulter-blue eyes that had lost their drive.

Guy said: "Things are changing, aren't they? Law's coming into the country and the laws are for the little men. You're trying to say that the time is past when you can grab what you want and hold it by force."

"I guess that's it. Ten years ago you'd have fought off this bunch that's coming and got clear away with it. You can't do it now. You fight them and drive them off, and they'll come back doubled. They'll keep coming back until they get you."

It was almost dark outside now. Almost dark and there wasn't much time left. Guy went out the door without a backward glance. Knox stood in the doorway, watching him. Guy roped a horse from the bunch in the corral and threw up his saddle. Red Daly called from the barn: "What's up, boss?"

Guy mounted, rode over until he was under the loft door. He said simply—"Take your orders from Knox for a while, Red."— and went away into the deepening gloom.

Knox called loudly into the yard: "Boys, no shooting unless I give the word!"

He went into the ranch office and took a gun and belt down from a nail on the wall, then belted it around his middle. He had a moment of self-doubt during which he wondered if he had done right, and then that was gone before the new assurance he had come into tonight. And he walked alone out into the yard to wait.

Perhaps if Knox had realized the complexity of the relationship between Freitag, Arnold, and Orvie, he would not have felt so sure. He had no way of knowing that Freitag's hold over the two was compounded of fear. He had no way of knowing that Jess intended to kill the sheriff, or that the sheriff intended to dispose of both Jess and Orvie by exposing their crimes.

So engrossed was he now with his own thoughts and troubles that he did not notice the change that had come into the air. It was hot, perhaps even more so than usual, but there was a difference, and it lay in the stickiness of the air.

He had a thought, which was that men are not so brave and reckless in bright light, so he yelled up at Red Daly, "Red, fork down a good-sized pile of hay, and then throw me the fork!"

Almost immediately he heard the dry crackling *thump* as a forkful of hay hit the ground, another, another.

The pile built up quickly before the barn, and, when Knox thought it was enough, he called: "All right! Now the fork."

He could hear the distant thunder of hoofs as he picked up the fork. He drove it deeply into the pile of dry hay and lifted. He carried this load and four others, all of them heavy, out away from the barn. Then he tossed the fork back in the general direction of the barn and got out a handful of matches.

Standing silently now, there was only one sound in his ears—the sound of rapidly approaching hoofs. It came to him then how foolish this was. Fifteen men, or thereabouts, were coming.

One hothead in the bunch could and would spoil everything. Gunfire would racket in the yard at Dollar, briefly, and Knox would die first. After that the crew would take over, and there would be hell to pay.

Knox turned and looked at the blackness of the slope behind the house. Guy was up there somewhere, and it might not be too late to call him back.

Guy Coulter was Dollar, not Knox. Let him come back and run this show.

But Knox didn't turn, and he didn't call. There comes a time when every man has to stand on his own two feet and do what he thinks is right. What he thinks is right isn't always so, but he does what he thinks he should anyway, and in that itself there is right enough.

Pounding along steadily, they swept into the lane and down toward the house. Knox's ears followed them, placed them, for in this light he could not see over twenty feet before him.

As they left the lane and started across the yard, Knox struck a match on the seat of his jeans and flung it into the pile.

The flare slowed them, and Freitag bellowed: "We want Guy for murder! No funny stuff now, or we'll blow the place to bits."

The posse pulled up in a roiling cloud of dust fifty feet away. Flame licked at the hay, and it flared like a torch, bathing the whole yard in its bright light.

Knox, standing spraddle-legged, said: "Let's see your warrant, Sheriff."

"To hell with that!" Freitag turned. "Boys, he's getting away. This is just a damned stall. Search the place."

Knox shook his head, having to raise his voice to be heard over the talking within the posse. "I wouldn't do that. This hay'll burn out quick. But right now, it makes plenty of light." He turned, yelled: "Red! Sing out!"

"Sure, boss. Right here. I got a bead on Freitag right now."

Knox called: "The rest of you. Sing out!"

They did, from all parts of the yard. But you couldn't see them. They were behind buildings, behind the woodpile, in the bunkhouse windows.

Knox said, his voice carrying well in the utter silence: "Bruce, I see you there. I see Ray, too. I see a lot of you that I know. Guy didn't hang Arch, and I can prove it."

Freitag sneered: "Big talk. Meantime Guy's getting away. If Guy didn't do it, he's got nothin' to lose surrenderin' to me."

Knox made himself grin. "Nothing but his life. Because you're the man that hung Arch. You and Jess Arnold and Orvie Gartrell."

There was an instant murmur of disbelief from the posse. The murmur swelled angrily. Someone shouted: "Cut the son down!"

Knox felt his own anger rising. He bawled. "Damn you, go ahead! *Go ahead!* Then try to find cover before our crew cuts you down!"

Bruce Adams yelled: "He's right! Watch yourselves!" And when the racket quieted a little, added: "He says he's got proof. Let's hear it before we try anything stupid."

There was a light murmur of assent from the crowd. Knox said loudly, holding out the metal tag: "This here was in Arch's hand when I found him this morning. I figured he'd pulled it off the back of the saddle he was sitting in when they hanged him. So I went to town and looked through the saddles in Orvie's stable. I found the one this came off of, and I found where Arch had scratched the letters F-R-I."

Freitag's voice beat against his. "The hell! You went down to Orvie's stable and pried the tag off yourself. Then you scratched the letters in the saddle." He turned to his posse. "You call that proof?"

Bruce Adams said reluctantly: "He's right, Knox. It ain't proof."

Knox saw that the hay pile fire was burning down. His time was running out. In another minute the light would be gone, this posse safe from the bullets of Dollar's crew. And when that happened, Knox knew he'd be the first to die.

He cried desperately: "There's something else that makes it proof! Someone saw Freitag and Orvie and Jess leave town at ten last night. They were leading an extra horse . . . saddled."

Bruce rode toward him. "You ain't lyin', Knox?"

"Hell no, I'm not lying."

Suddenly something struck Knox's forehead. He put up a hand and wiped it away. Water. He frowned with puzzlement, and then another drop struck him. It was impossible. But it seemed to be happening. Rain?

The temper of the crowd was touchy, but that rain, if rain it was, would give Knox a tremendous psychological advantage.

Bruce Adams said: "Who saw them, Knox?"

"Nell DeAndrea."

Suddenly all hell broke loose. The rain came in a torrent, in huge, splattering drops mixed with hail. They made a thunder against the dusty ground, drowned the fire almost instantly. In the utter darkness then, Bruce Adams yelled: "Let's find out about this! Freitag, another day won't hurt. Guy won't run."

It was hard to hear, and all the men in the posse were shouting. Freitag's voice came through the uproar: "All right! All right, you damned bunch of yellowbellies. I can't take him by myself. Orvie! Jess! Let's get the hell out of here."

Knox heard the run of their horses' hoofs going across the yard, entering the lane.

At first he could feel only relief, the drain of strength that is the aftermath of such intolerable strain. Dollar's crew came out of hiding, mixed with the posse, and they all turned their faces up toward the sky, laughing like kids as the rain soaked and battered them.

Some little thing was troubling Knox, and for a moment he couldn't tell what it was. Lightning split the sky, and thunder rolled after it. The smell of the land, freshly wetted, was good after so long a drought. Knox scowled, troubled.

And then, very suddenly he had it. Knox's own story, the tag and saddle might be worthless without Nell DeAndrea's story to back them up. But with Nell's testimony, they'd be enough not only to defeat Freitag's plan to seize Dollar, but enough to hang Freitag and Orvie and Jess as well.

It still seemed fantastic that Nell could be in danger, until the realization struck Knox like a blow. *If they could hang a man in cold blood for no reason at all, they are capable of killing a woman, too.*

His voice was a scream against the thunder of the storm, and he was running: "Red! Frank! Dutch! Dollar crew! Saddle up and come with me!"

He found the corral by instinct in the darkness, found a rope stiffened by rain on the gate. He made a fast loop, and it sailed out into the vaguely visible, milling bunch of excited horses. He pulled the horse in, pulled him out through the gate. He got his own saddle off the horse he had ridden earlier and slapped it onto the back of this fresh one. He bridled the freshly caught horse and swung instantly to the saddle.

Dollar's crew was now streaming into the corral, driven by the urgency of his voice. Knox shouted: "Red, take half of them and go to Chimney Rock! Nell's either there or at Arch Dorrance's place. I'll go to Arch Dorrance's. But, for Lord's sake, Red, hurry! Nell is the only witness that can hurt Freitag. And if Freitag could hang Arch, he sure as the devil ain't above killing a woman."

Because he couldn't wait until the crew had caught horses

and saddled, Knox spurred his horse and thundered out of the yard alone.

XII

The first fury of the rain beat against him as he rode. He was soaked clear to his hide before he had gone a quarter mile. The skies seemed to be trying to empty in an hour what they had been withholding all summer, but by the time Knox came to the halfway mark, an old, abandoned homestead cabin, the storm had settled down to a light, steady downpour that would do more real good than a dozen flash floods.

Over on his right, Knox could hear the rising murmur of the creek, running for the first time in two months. He might have enjoyed it, but for the terrible fear that sent chill after chill running down his spine.

The rain would clean out all the stinking pools in Dollar and Wild Horse Creek; it would renew the springs on Dry Ridge, would obviate Dollar's need to seize Wild Horse Ridge. New grass would grow, and Dollar cattle would fatten on it.

Dollar would live at peace with its neighbors, and, eventually, Rudy's death and Arch's and the events that had led to them would be forgotten.

But what good would all of that be if something happened to Nell? Knox faced that, hard as it was, and realized now what he should have realized months ago. He loved Nell. He didn't even want to face a life that didn't hold her, too.

This afternoon's kiss had something to do with this realization. Her imminent danger completed the process.

Immediately upon leaving Dollar, Knox had appraised this horse he was riding, had estimated its stamina. He judged the horse could go at a dead run the seven miles to Wild Horse Creek, the extra mile and a half from the forks to Dorrance's ranch. So he sank his spurs mercilessly and the horse, excited anyway by the rain, stretched itself out and ran.

The distance seemed to pass with a slowness that was agonizing. Knox tried to judge how far ahead Freitag would be, but there was no way for him to tell how many minutes had passed between the time the sheriff had departed and the time he himself had left.

He consoled himself with the realization that Freitag's, Orvie's, and Jess's horses would not be as fresh as his own. He also consoled himself with the thought: *Freitag doesn't know she went to Dorrance's.*

But supposing the sheriff caught her on the road? That would make Freitag's task ridiculously easy. Kill her with a blow to the head. Whip her horse into running away, and then crowd him off the road so that the buggy was wrecked. Who could then prove it had been murder?

Knox's long mouth thinned out, drew away from his teeth. Rain streamed down off the brim of his hat, blowing into his unheeding face. He spoke aloud, his voice hardly audible through his clenched teeth: "If he hurts her, I'll put a bullet in his belly!"

Slowly, slowly the miles streamed past. Once, Knox thought he heard a shout behind. But he paid it no heed. Time was too important to waste even a minute of it waiting for the others to catch up.

His horse was steaming now. Steaming and streaming rain. Its hoofs, rising off the wet clay road, threw huge gobs of mud behind. Lightning flashed, and Knox saw the plain imprints of three horses before him.

Knox reached the forks, passed the tree, shrouded in darkness and rain where Arch had been hanged. The road forked immediately thereafter, the right fork heading toward Chimney Rock, the left heading up Wild Horse Creek and joining the main road after a quarter mile.

Thundering up to this fork, Knox tried to make up his mind. Very likely, Nell DeAndrea was still at Dorrance's place.

Yet he could not be sure, and he could not see the ground in the darkness, could not see the prints of the horses he was pursuing. Behind him, perhaps a quarter or a half a mile, Dollar's crew came with instructions to split here at this fork in the road.

Knox's horse barely slowed as he made his decision. If he was wrong, he'd never stop blaming himself.

He turned up Wild Horse Creek and headed for Arch Dorrance's place.

Freitag led out from Dollar at a hard run, with Orvie and Jess following perhaps 100 yards behind at first. They caught up slowly as they rode. Jess was trembling with his terror, for all his terrified mind could see was a rope and a dangling carcass turning slowly in the breeze. Only that dangling carcass wasn't Arch anymore. It was Jess himself, shapeless as a sack of grain.

When he was but ten yards behind Freitag, he yelled: "What are we going to do now?"

Freitag's horse was flinging huge gobs of mud into the air behind him, and Jess pulled right a little to avoid them. Freitag hipped around in his saddle. A flash of lightning illuminated his face, showed his streaming mustache and his white teeth beneath it. The lightning flash died and Freitag's voice came back: "Find that damned girl. Either we get her, or we stretch a rope."

Jess screamed, his stomach churning: "You can't do that!"

Freitag laughed loudly and wildly. "I can, and I will! And you'll help me."

Jess began to tremble. *Oh, Judas,* he thought, *how deep can a man get in trouble?* He knew where the DeAndrea girl was. She was up at Dorrance's place. He'd seen her turn in there as he

86

reached the forks late this afternoon. But Freitag didn't know. And that put the burden of decision in this directly upon Jess's shoulders.

Orvie shouted: "You going to town then?"

Freitag didn't answer, for the answer was obvious. Neither Freitag nor Orvie knew where the girl was. Only Jess knew. Freitag was assuming she was in town, and, if Jess kept still, her life might be saved.

Except for one slight circumstance, Jess might not have had to make the decision alone. If Orvie had not been in such a hurry this afternoon, everything might have been different. But Orvie had elected to ride out of town immediately, while Jess had stayed to go through the drawers of the sheriff's desk. And so it had been Jess alone who had, from a high vantage point on the road before he reached the forks, seen Nell DeAndrea turning her buggy into the lane at Dorrance's.

The miles drove behind with frightening rapidity. Jess fought with what little conscience he had, and won the fight. He'd not hang to save the life of a girl he scarcely knew. To Jess, his own life was more important than anything else.

Long before they reached the forks, he ranged up beside the sheriff and shouted: "Nell DeAndrea ain't in town, Freitag! She's up at Dorrance's. I saw her turn in there this afternoon."

Freitag was silent, but, when they came to the forks, his decision was made, for he turned left and took the upcreek road toward Dorrance's. Nell might have stayed but a short time, then driven back to town. But Jess knew that wasn't likely. Sue Dorrance would be wholly demoralized by Arch's death. And Nell would probably spend the night with her.

Jess had no idea how Freitag intended to work this. He only knew that Nell would have to die.

They came into Dorrance's lane at a run, and swung down into the mud off their horses.

Nell's buggy sat directly before the house, the shafts resting on the ground. Freitag shouted: "Orvie, go get her horse and hitch up! Jess, you stay here!"

He went up onto the porch and knocked on the door. Nell answered it, and Jess heard Freitag ask in lowered tones, but worriedly: "Nell, how is Missus Dorrance?"

"Sleeping at last. It was a hard blow to her."

"Then you can leave?"

"I don't think I should. Why should I leave?"

"Your pa's been hurt. Pretty bad." He kept his voice low-pitched so that it barely carried to where Jess was standing.

He saw Nell's face go pale, saw her lips part with her sudden intake of breath. Her eyes were wide with fear. "What happened?" she managed to whisper.

"Horse fell with him. Orvie's hitching up your buggy. Get your coat and we'll ride back to town with you." Freitag hesitated, finally saying: "I don't think I'd wake Missus Dorrance, Nell. Another shock wouldn't do her any good."

"I suppose not." Nell left the door, running, and came back in an instant with a yellow slicker thrown around her. She said: "I hate to leave Sue."

"Sure. I know. I'll send somebody back to stay with her."

Suddenly Jess felt a little sick as he thought of Nell, her head bashed in, lying in the mud at the roadside, which was where she'd be before half an hour was gone. Jess knew a fleeting regret that he was not more of a man, then finally shrugged fatalistically.

Nell ran out and climbed into the buggy, which Orvie had finished hitching up. Freitag said: "Jess, go back in the house and blow out the lamp. You can catch up."

Jess nodded his assent, glad at least that he would not have to witness the killing. He stood on the porch and watched as the buggy, trailed by Freitag and Orvie, splashed up the lane.

How long would they wait? Not very long, he guessed. Freitag, knowing that pursuit couldn't be far behind, would only go out of earshot before he stopped Nell's buggy.

Jess shivered and went into the house on tiptoe to blow out the lamp.

Knox heard a single, shrill scream above the howl of the wind and the beat of hoofs beneath him. The sound had almost the effect of a knife plunged into him. It brought a pain that was sharp and helpless. And it brought fury unmatched by anything he had ever known before.

Ordinarily mild and peace-loving, Knox turned instantly into a machine with only the urge to kill motivating it. There was that scream, and then a shouted curse. Knox's spurs went into his horse's sides, drawing blood, forcing from the animal a startled, pain-filled leap forward. Knox realized that his gun was in his hand, and he had no recollection of drawing it.

Ahead of him loomed a buggy, stopped in the road. And off to one side, Knox saw the light blur of Nell's skirt, as she ran through the high brush. A darker blob of something behind her told Knox she was being pursued. His hand yanked the reins over, and the horse plunged off the road and into the brush. Knox's gun came up, and he snapped a shot at the man chasing Nell.

The man stopped, melted into the brush without a trace. Knox rode after Nell, calling: "Nell! It's Knox!"

He flung himself from his horse, and was beside her. She would have come into his arms, but roughly he pushed her to the ground, saying harshly: "They're not through yet. There's nothing but hanging ahead for the three of them unless they can get you, and they won't give up just yet."

She was sobbing, almost silently but with a certain hysteria. Knox knelt beside her, trying to pierce the darkness with his eyes. Freitag was here, somewhere, the most dangerous of the three. Perhaps he was even now but a dozen feet away, concealed by brush and shadows, drawing his bead on the two of them.

The lightness, which Knox had thought was Nell's skirt, was in reality her slicker. Beneath that, she wore a dress of some dark material. Knox whispered into her ear: "Get that slicker off. Quick."

She shrugged out of the slicker, and Knox wadded it into a ball and stood up silently. He walked carefully a dozen yards, then hung the slicker on a tall clump of brush, arranging it so that it might be mistaken for a woman, standing there.

He was frantic with worry for her safety when he got back to Nell. She put her lips close to his ear, and started to whisper something, but Knox gripped her arm savagely, and she held her silence.

Now there was just the waiting. If they could wait long enough, Dollar's crew would be along. The buggy out there in the road would halt them, and after that it would be all over for Freitag.

Perhaps Freitag was realizing this, too, for he called: "Knox? Is that you?"

Knox didn't answer. The voice had come from the direction of the road, perhaps halfway to it. Farther off to his left, he heard a twig *snap*, and placed Orvie by that. Where Jess was, only heaven knew. Three of them advancing through the brush even now. And Dollar's crew wouldn't arrive in time. Nell, trembling violently, was going to break down and begin weeping soon now. Weeping with fear and terror. When she did, she'd give away their position.

So it was move ahead, and find Freitag, or let the sheriff find him. Freitag would never believe Knox had left Nell. So, perhaps for now at least, Nell would be safer if he left her. And the rattle of gunfire would bring Dollar's cowpunchers on the double.

Knox put his mouth against Nell's ear. "Lie here and be quiet," he ordered.

She stirred with protest, and he gripped her arm tightly.

"Don't argue now. Lie here and be quiet. I'm going to draw them off."

Before she could protest again, he got up and moved away, very carefully for the first fifty feet, then more noisily, allowing his boots to make a sucking sound as he pulled them out of the mud at each step, allowing brush to scratch against him as he walked.

Almost at once a bullet sought him in the inky dark, clipping brush twigs inches from his face.

But he had seen the flash of that. Instinct brought his gun up, centered its muzzle on the flash that had bloomed over there on his right. He thumbed back the hammer and let the shot go, and then, without waiting for the result of it, threw himself violently to the ground.

It was slick and muddy, but better that than the two quick-triggered shots that Orvie Gartrell threw at his gun flash.

Knox got up, running, crouched low, heading for the road and making a path of sound in that direction.

As suddenly as he had run, he stopped, and waited, his breathing harsh. He put his left hand up over his mouth to quiet that.

But his ruse was working. On right and left behind him he heard their crashing movement as they tried to cut him off.

Hang it, he wished he could guess where Jess Arnold was. Maybe on the road with the buggy. Maybe closer than that. Jess was the imponderable in this fight that Knox had to worry about but couldn't plan against.

Quietly, making his course by the sounds Freitag made, Knox moved to the right, now intercepting his own interceptor. He saw Freitag as a looming shape five feet away, going past him, and flung up his gun. The hammer *clicked* as it came back, and the lumpy, barely visible shape of the sheriff halted and whirled around.

Knox squeezed down on the trigger, having no time to move after that before the sheriff's bullet caught him in the thigh. The shock of it was like the blow of a giant fist, and it took the leg out from under him and dumped him in the mud, wondering briefly at the quickness of it.

The sheriff, though, was still, utterly still. *Unconscious? Or only playing 'possum? Or dead?*

Orvie made a crashing sound as he approached, and now Knox heard the dim beat of hoofs in the distance, which Orvie had probably not heard yet. Knox called—"Over here, Orvie, damn you."—wanting Orvie himself before someone else got him. "Over here, Orvie, you dirty son-of-a-bitch!"

A wildness was in Knox that was new to him. A fighting wildness that wanted to destroy, to kill, to batter and pound. The sheriff stirred a little where he lay, and Knox threw his body over onto the sheriff and brought his gun down in a savage, chopping motion to Freitag's neck. Again to his head.

Orvie yelled: "Hey . . . !" And loomed over Knox, his gun shadowy in his big fist. Knox shot, shot again as Orvie's body came plunging against him.

Orvie knocked him backwards, wrenching and twisting his wounded thigh. The pain dizzied Knox, made his brain reel. And Orvie wasn't dead. He was twisting, trying to get his gun around.

Knox's gun still rested, its muzzle against him. So Knox thumbed back the hammer and pulled the trigger. The hammer came down with a harmless *click* against an empty chamber.

Yet Orvie still moved, still struggled to come around. Knox felt consciousness slipping away under the pain of that twisted leg, perhaps from loss of blood.

Orvie's gun muzzle punched him in the chest, and he slapped it away frantically, trying to club his own gun against Orvie's skull. He had no knowledge of the men that were thundering up around the two of them. He could only concentrate on Orvie, whose monstrous strength refused to die, whose gun still held four bullets, any one of which could spell an end to this.

And then, from nowhere, a running, sobbing shape appeared. Nell flung herself at Orvie, clawing his face, by her very fury turning Orvie's effort from Knox to herself.

Giving Knox his chance, which was to come to his knees, and club his gun muzzle viciously downward against Orvie's upturned forehead.

Red Daly's hand gripped Knox's elbows, pulling him up, and Knox began to fight him, too, until Red's admiring, soothing voice said: "Hey, kid! This is Red. Your fight's over."

"No. There's Jess yet."

"We'll get him. He's too fat to run very far."

Red let him go and Knox fell down, unable to stand his weight on that bad leg. He could hear his own voice cursing, and then Nell was down there in the mud beside him, crying out: "You're hurt! Where is it, Knox? Where is it, darling?"

Someone in the crew had found a lantern in the buggy, and now brought it, running. Red Daly took the strips Nell tore from her petticoat and made a tight bandage for Knox's thigh.

He could hear Nell talking, sometimes tenderly, and for him alone, sometimes almost hysterically as she told of how Freitag had stopped the buggy, pulled her out, and tried to kill her. "He was going to kill me and put me back in the buggy. Then he was going to whip the buggy horse into a run and crowd him off the road so that the buggy would overturn. He said it would look like an accident."

Someone helped Knox into the buggy, and Nell got in beside him, pulling his head over onto her shoulder. He felt like a fool for being so weak, but it was pleasant too. He said: "Nell?"

"What?" There was unaccustomed shyness in her voice, as though she knew what he would say next.

He got his hands up behind her head and pulled her down against him. There was weakness in Knox, but her kiss made him feel strong again. He sat up and took the reins from her unprotesting hands. And clucked to the buggy horse.

Moving along the road toward town, he said, grinning: "We ought to do that oftener."

"Yes, Knox."

"Legally."

She was smiling, too. "Any way at all."

"We'll have to wait until morning to get married." He pulled the horse to a halt and drew her into his arms. "But we don't have to wait for this." And he lowered his head to kiss her again.

★ ★ ★ ★ ★

Shadow of the Gun

★ ★ ★ ★ ★

I

Dark, solid gray was the sky. Gentle, steady rain pattered down, slanting slightly from the north on an easy wind. It ran in steady streams from the eaves of Whitewater's frame buildings. It turned the wide streets to a sea of sticky yellow clay. A comfortable rain if you could stay inside. A cold and miserable one if you could not.

But a rain that would bring up the grass, that would green the trees and brush. A rain that would soak into the thirsty ground and feed the springs that kept the country living during the summer months.

Wade Daugherty sat in his swivel chair in the sheriff's office and listened to the steady patter of it on the corrugated roof above him. He stared moodily out into the dripping street.

From where he sat, he could see the huge, awkward shape of the Great Western Hotel across the street, its verandah empty because of the weather. He could see the bleak, sodden horses racked before the Mesa Saloon next door. Beyond that, he could see Prior's store. Three places where men could gather and talk—Prior's cracker barrel, the Mesa Saloon bar, and the hotel lobby.

Wade knew that in all three places men were gathered. And he knew the subject of their conversation. Curt McVey was coming back.

A shadow crossed his field of vision and paused before his door. Jesse Kellman came in, rain dripping from the wide brim of his hat and running off his yellow slicker. He stamped mud off his boots just inside the door, wheezing and blowing like a winded horse. Wade put his feet on the floor and reached for his pipe. The swivel chair *squeaked* its audible protest at the sudden movement.

Kellman shucked out of his slicker, peered at Wade from beneath his bushy brows as he wiped a drop of rain from the tip of his long, hooked nose. "You heard?"

Wade made the slightest of sour smiles and took time to pack his pipe deliberately before he answered. "Heard? About Curt, you mean?" He shrugged and touched a match to the bowl of his pipe. He puffed carefully until he had a glowing coal, and then dropped the match into the brass spittoon at the side of the desk.

He was a tall, loosely muscled man who sat with complete relaxation and stared thoughtfully at his visitor. His face was somewhat angular, yet even after the long winter it still retained its leathery, sun-bronzed color. If you looked closely, you could see a few gray hairs at his temples although he was barely thirty. Someday he would look distinguished. Now he only looked competent, calm, and tough. His eyes were a pale blue and, fixed so steadily upon Kellman, had the effect of making him uneasy and slightly angry.

Kellman asked belligerently: "So what are you going to do about it?"

Wade took his pipe from his mouth and transferred his gaze from Kellman to the bowl of his blackened pipe. He said mildly: "Nothing. What should I do?"

"You need me to tell you that?"

Something flickered brightly in Wade Daugherty's eyes. He got deliberately to his feet. Kellman took a backward step, and then looked angry because he had.

Wade said: "I don't need anybody to tell me what to do.

Because there's nothing I can do. Curt McVey is coming back. But he's not wanted here, nor any place else so far as I know. Until he breaks the law, he can come and go as he pleases. Does that answer your question?"

"He killed my father."

Wade argued patiently: "That was three years ago. Your old man drew his iron first. The coroner turned Curt loose."

Kellman looked at him with bitter irony. He had aged in the last three years. He had steadied down. Right now he looked like old Ross Kellman had looked years before. He had the same arrogance, the same intolerance. Yet there must have been something lacking in his make-up that had been present in the old man. Because after the old man's death at Curt McVey's hands, Jesse and Sam Kellman had seemed satisfied with what they had, and had not tried to extend K Diamond's boundaries.

Kellman said: "And that was justice, I suppose? Curt McVey was a gunman. Yanking his iron and playing cards were the only two things he knew how to do. He kept his hands soft as a woman's. Dad was different. He worked cattle. His hands were stiff and he had rheumatism in his arms." He snorted contemptuously. "You call that a fair fight?"

Wade shook his head. "You're forgetting something. I'm the sheriff of this county. I bring in the lawbreakers. I don't try them. If you've got a complaint, go to the coroner. Take your complaint to him. I arrested Curt ten minutes after the shooting, and, when I did, my job was done."

Kellman stared at him angrily for a moment. "So McVey comes back to Whitewater and nobody bothers him, is that it? He's a killer, but that's all right." His tone lowered until it was scarcely more than a hoarse whisper. "Daugherty, I'll tell you something. You let McVey stay in Whitewater more than twenty-four hours and I'll kill him."

Wade made an almost imperceptible shrug.

Kellman went on: "Not with a holster gun. I won't commit suicide like Dad did. I'll get him with a shotgun and I'll forget all about the rules."

Wade shrugged again. "Do that and I'll come after you, Jesse. Like I would after any killer."

Kellman stared at him and growled at last: "By Judas, you would, wouldn't you?"

Wade nodded.

Kellman reached for his slicker. "All right. I'll do it another way then. I'll do it so you'll never be able to pin it on me."

"It's been tried. But it doesn't often succeed. Remember that, Jesse."

"I'll remember it." Kellman shrugged into his yellow slicker. He put his hand on the doorknob but he didn't go out. He just looked at Wade in his odd, angry way. Wade could almost see the thoughts churning in his head through the open windows of his eyes. Kellman said: "You're a damned fool, Wade."

"Maybe."

"A damned fool. Curt's coming back is going to cost you more than it'll cost any of the rest of us. Maybe. . . ."

Wade's eyes were suddenly ice. The color went out of his face. But his voice was calm enough, except that it held a restrained intensity. He interrupted: "That's enough from you. Get out of here."

He took a step toward Jesse Kellman.

Suddenly Kellman grinned. "Sure, Wade, sure," he muttered, and went out into the rain.

Wade went back and sat down at his desk. He laid his hands flat on its top and looked at them. Big hands, with square-tipped fingers and large knuckles. He picked them up and saw that they were trembling. Angrily he shoved them into his pockets.

He put his booted feet up onto the desk top. Those last words of Kellman's kept echoing in his mind. *You're a damned fool, Wade. Curt's coming back is going to cost you more than it'll cost any of the rest of us.* ... And that *maybe* Kellman had been starting when Wade's words had silenced him—Wade knew he could finish what Kellman had been about to say, and thought of it made a sickness come to his mind and made him violently angry. *Maybe Ellen Santangelo will go back to him now. Maybe he'll take her away from you like he did before.* ...

Wade yanked his hands from his pockets. He seized a chunk of ore that he used for a paperweight and flung it violently across the room. Afterwards he looked ashamed. And calm again.

But his thoughts went on. *Why did Curt have to come back? What was there in Whitewater for him?* The answer to that came quickly enough. Ellen Santangelo.

Not that Curt ever really wanted her. Permanently anyway. To Curt, women were pleasurable and necessary, but none of them would ever hold him long.

Scowling, Wade regarded the dismal street. He saw Kellman reach the far side, stamp mud from his boots on the walk, and turn. There was a visible grin on Kellman's face. The man went into the Mesa Saloon.

The rain came down steadily and relentlessly. Wade thought of Curt, riding somewhere in this rain. Riding hunched over, slickered and cold, heading for Whitewater. Wade felt trapped.

For three years now the county had been relatively peaceful, but Wade had a feeling that Curt's coming would change all that. Curt was the kind that brought trouble with him wherever he went.

Already it was beginning. With Jesse Kellman's threat to kill Curt.

A shadow passed before Wade's vision. His eyes focused on it and he saw old Doc Sayers passing, head down against the slanting rain. The man staggered a little, stopped, and put his hand on the knob of the sheriff's door.

Doc was small and oldish, a gray little man whose gray life had driven him to the bottle as it had driven so many before him. He never really got blind drunk, but he kept enough liquor inside him all the time to keep him in a kind of pleasant haze. Doc was the county coroner, and years ago he had been a doctor until the liquor he drank interfered with his practice. So he'd run for county coroner and folks had elected him because they figured he couldn't hurt dead men no matter how drunk he got.

He came in and peered owlishly at Wade through his thick-lensed glasses that had fogged with steam from the heat inside. He took them off and wiped them with a soiled white handkerchief that he fished from his pocket. His eyes were a pale gray, very vague, but friendly for all of that. Helpless, confused eyes.

Wade was reminded of a very young fawn he'd seen once, close up. The fawn's eyes had possessed the same quality of uncomprehending helplessness. Wade smiled. He said: "Hi, Doc."

Doc's voice was squeaky as he adjusted his glasses. "Hello, Sheriff. It's a miserable day. Miserable." He shivered and crossed the room to the stove. He wore no slicker and his coat was damp. He backed against the stove that was only slightly warm. Steam and a wet wool smell rose from his clothes.

"I hear Curt McVey is coming back. Reckon there's anything to it?"

Wade felt a touch of irritation. Curt McVey. He'd heard nothing else since morning when young Tommy Rennick had come fogging in from the Cañon Creek road, yelling it at the top of his lungs. His story was that McVey had spent the night at Rennick's.

Wade said: "I guess it's true enough. Rennick's kid brought

the news this morning. Curt ought to ride in just about any time, depending on how long he fooled around at Rennick's today."

"Spent the night there, did he?"

Wade nodded.

"Going to run Curt out again?"

Wade said patiently: "I didn't run him out before. He left of his own accord."

Doc smiled vaguely. "Yes. I remember now. Why's he coming back?"

Wade shrugged. He'd asked that question of himself, but he wasn't entirely satisfied with the answer.

Doc kept watching him and waiting for his answer, but Wade didn't give it. Doc's eyes lost some of their vagueness and you could almost see his mind going to work. Doc said: "He'll make trouble. He's the kind that always makes trouble."

"I know. It's already started."

Doc left the stove, chafing his hands in front of him. His stomach bulged in a slight paunch and there were food stains on the front of his black serge vest. He came over to the desk, looking down at Wade timidly. He hesitated for a moment over what he wanted to say. At last he cleared his throat and said: "Your Ellen is a good girl. Three years have likely changed her and I doubt if she's scatter-brained any more. Give yourself credit, Sheriff, for being able to hold her."

Wade felt his irritation growing. It showed in his frown, in his hardening eyes.

Doc said hastily: "No offense, Sheriff."

Wade grinned at him. "No. No offense." He added to himself: *Damn a small town anyway.*

Doc shuffled his feet, looking down at them. He studied Wade with his vague, pale eyes. He mumbled: "Well, I'll be going." But he didn't go.

Wade knew what he wanted and finally said: "You need something to tide you over till the county warrants arrive, Doc?"

Relief relaxed the lines of Doc's face. He smiled and the smile made a change in him that was wonderful to see. "I hated to ask, Sheriff."

"Forget it." Wade fished in his pocket and brought out a couple of silver dollars. He handed them to Doc. Doc mumbled his thanks and scurried to the door. He went out into the rain and crossed at a shambling run to the Mesa Saloon. Wade thought—*I shouldn't do that.*—knowing the money would be spent for whiskey. Quickly he argued to himself—*Why the devil shouldn't I?*—then promptly forgot Doc.

For a man had come into his field of vision. A man riding down the middle of Main.

There was a deceptiveness about the rider's size. He didn't appear large but Wade knew he was. He was almost as tall as the sheriff and a whole lot heavier. Yet he appeared almost slight.

His horse was mud-splattered to the knees and showed the effects of hard usage. There was a rifle in the man's saddle boot, its scarred stock protruding, and a blanket roll tied behind his saddle.

He wore a battered black hat, a short sheepskin, and tight chaps that were shiny with grease and scarred with wear. Most noticeable, however, were his two guns protruding at a sharp angle from his lean thighs.

Wade would have known him instantly at twice this distance. For he was Curt McVey.

Wade walked over to the window just as McVey reined his horse in at the rail. McVey dismounted stiffly and looped his reins around the rail. He looked up, saw Wade watching him, and made a cheerful, mocking grin.

For the briefest instant, wild anger flared in Wade Daugherty. But he brought it under control and the face he showed McVey as he came in was as expressionless as a piece of stone.

McVey slammed the door behind him. He grinned and said amiably: "Nothing changes, does it, Wade?"

Wade grunted. "Some things do. Others don't. What the devil do you want in Whitewater?"

McVey's grin never wavered. "That's no way to treat an old friend. I got homesick."

Close up like this, you could see how big he was. But his weight was evenly distributed in smooth, hard muscles. Wade wondered how he'd developed those muscles, for he never worked. Curt thumbed his hat back on his head, exposing a mop of curly black hair. His eyes were dark, laughing. He looked so damned harmless sometimes.

Wade said: "Jesse Kellman was just in."

Curt's grin faded momentarily, then came back brighter than before. "So?"

"He says he'll kill you if you're in town more than twenty-four hours."

"He can try." Curt's grin had faded entirely.

Wade said: "He won't face you. It'll be with a shotgun . . . from behind or when you're not expecting it."

Curt repeated: "He can try."

Wade could see the change that three years had made in Curt. He could see that the eyes were harder, colder. He could see that Curt's mouth had thinned, that there were new lines of cruelty around it. These things were mostly hidden when Curt was smiling, but he wasn't smiling now. And the shadow of the gun was upon his face.

II

With anger rising in him, Wade Daugherty turned and walked back to his desk. Holding his pipe over the brass spittoon, he knocked it against the heel of his palm and ashes spilled out of it.

The law said that McVey was guiltless in the killing of Ross Kellman three years before. He could come and go as he pleased, so long as he made no trouble. Trouble? Wade smiled grimly. Curt would make nothing else so long as he stayed here and his expression told Wade plainly that he was well aware of how much trouble his presence in Whitewater County would cause. He gloried in it.

Wade asked harshly: "What do you want, Curt?"

"I said I was homesick." Curt's mocking smile gave the lie to his words.

"I asked you a question. Hang you, give me a straight answer."

Curt's expression seemed to settle and a slight flush colored his neck. He growled: "Maybe I figure this country owes me something."

Wade stared at him. Maybe the country did owe Curt something. There'd been a man-size range war brewing three years ago and Curt had stopped it with a single, well-placed bullet. He'd killed old Ross Kellman and had stopped K Diamond's greedy grabbing of neighboring range. But not before Kellman got part of Ed Sontag's Mill Iron and a chunk of Rennick's place.

Curt had stopped more than Kellman's grab for range. With the same bullet he'd stopped the resistance that was beginning to grow among the smaller ranchers. Everyone figured Kellman's death had saved a lot of lives in the long run and perhaps that was why Curt had got off so easily.

Somehow, though, Wade Daugherty had never been able to cast Curt McVey in the rôle of the country's savior. Yet that was the rôle he had played.

Wade asked coldly: "What do you think the country owes you and how do you plan to collect?"

He was surprised at the bitterness that came into Curt's face, surprised at the anger that flared so suddenly in his dark eyes. Curt asked harshly: "You know how a man lives who lives by his guns?"

Wade shook his head silently.

Curt said savagely: "Hotel rooms, dirty and smelly. Restaurant meals you wouldn't feed the hogs in Whitewater County. Men that cringe and fawn over you while they wait for you to do things that are too dirty for them to do themselves. Between jobs watching your back, waiting for some lousy punk to put a bullet into it." He was almost snarling now. "And women. All kinds of women from the married tramps that play up to you because their men are afraid of you to the dance-hall girls that'd sell you out for a ten-dollar bill. There's only one end to it. You get shot, or you run afoul of the law. And nobody gives a damn."

Wade looked at him soberly. He said: "You've gone pretty sour, haven't you?" He watched the ugliness fade from Curt's face, watched the mocking smile return. He knew a sudden chill of uneasiness. It was as though Curt had changed from one man to an entirely different one right there before his eyes.

Except for the ugliness he had glimpsed in Curt, Wade might have been sorry for him. He said: "So you've made up your mind? You're going to stay?"

Curt nodded, and Wade shrugged. He had a feeling that Curt had come to his office for a very definite reason and wondered what it was. He said: "All right. Suit yourself. But take a warning. Jesse Kellman is laying for you and he'll kill you if he can. Rennick and Sontag will try to use you to get back the range they lost to K Diamond three years ago. A lot of people will likely be sorry if you stay. Including yourself, maybe."

"And including you?" Curt's grin was sardonic. "How is Ellen, by the way?"

Wade could feel his face darkening, so plain was Curt's

implication. He could feel, too, a growing tension within himself. As though something were going to happen over which he would have no control.

But he kept his voice steady and patient as he said: "She's fine. We're going to be married the First of May."

Some things you sensed and some you saw. Wade sensed the tightening of Curt's muscles, the imperceptible shift of the man's weight to the balls of his feet. He saw the plain sneer that came to Curt's mouth. Curt said, deliberately taunting: "You hope you'll be married the First of May. But now that I'm here, you're not sure any more, are you? So you'd like to move me on. You keep remembering how it was between Ellen and me. You're afraid it'll be that way again. That's the real reason you want me out of town, isn't it, Wade?" Curt made a suggestive leer. "Is Ellen still as lush as she used to be?"

Wade closed the space between them with two swift, lunging strides. A hard, bony left went out and smashed against Curt's mouth, driving him back, driving him away in a shuffling, backward run that stopped only when he crashed into the wall.

Wade would have stopped then perhaps, for an awareness of his surroundings and position came to him with a shock— awareness that Curt had deliberately baited him into just this situation.

But Curt pushed himself away from the wall, laughing evilly. He made no move at all toward his guns. He came cat-footing across the floor in a half crouch toward Wade, his attitude plainly saying that it could not stop now. A trickle of blood ran from one corner of his mouth. His eyes glittered. "Wade," he whispered, "I'm going to enjoy this."

Carefully he came, light-footed and easy. When he was but five feet away, he lunged, with speed that Wade would not have believed possible had he not seen it himself. Curt's left fist sank into Wade's middle and his right bounced with stunning force off Wade's high forehead.

Wade went backward, struggling for balance. Curt followed, swinging viciously, connecting twice.

The wall stopped Wade as it had stopped Curt. With his back to it, he met Curt's wildly vicious swings with countering punches of his own, and stayed there until the sickness went out of his belly, until the ringing stopped in his head. Curt might be a gunman. But he was also a fighter. His fists were hard and solid and there was enough weight behind them to knock out a man if they landed just right.

Wade pushed himself away from the wall. He blocked one of Curt's blows with a forearm, then slammed a hard right to Curt's nose. He could see the tears that sprang to Curt's eyes, and followed Curt's instinctive backward step with a forward one of his own. He swung a left, followed it with a savage right hook that landed flushly on the point of Curt's jaw. Curt staggered.

Wade bored in fiercely, raining blows with vicious concentration into Curt's face and body, driving him back, forcing him to give ground. With but a yard between him and the window, Curt stopped and made a stand.

But Wade had too much momentum, and too much fury in him to be stopped now. He drove a reckless right at Curt, one that lifted Curt bodily from the floor and slammed him backward against the office window. There was a *crash* of breaking glass, and then Curt was rolling on the wet sidewalk outside.

Wade lunged through the broken window. Curt came to his knees, grabbing belatedly and clumsily for one of his guns. Wade swung a vicious kick, and the gun went spinning into the mud of the street. Curt howled involuntarily with the pain in his wrist.

Then he got up, grinning triumphantly through his battered lips. Wade knew suddenly that this had turned out precisely as

Curt had planned it. Yet he could not help himself as he moved in and swung the finishing blow at Curt's jaw. All the force of his anger was behind it, and like the last blow it lifted Curt slightly and drove him back. He lit in the mud of the street on his shoulder blades and lay completely still.

Wade stood on the walk, legs spraddled, panting hoarsely. He became aware that there was an audience to this, perhaps a dozen men who had crossed the muddy street from the Mesa Saloon and the Great Western Hotel. Sontag was among them, a huge man with yellow, uncut hair that made small curls on his neck and around his ears. There was anger in Sontag's face, anger in the faces of two or three of the others. Kellman was grinning widely, triumphantly. The townsmen were only interested as they would be in any fight, and not vitally touched by it as were the ranchers, large and small.

Sontag grunted something to his friends, and three of them went over to Curt. They lifted him between them. Sontag looked at Wade, hostility plain in his eyes. "You charging him with anything?"

Wade shook his head. It was plain to him now exactly what had happened. Curt, ever sly, had come into his office with the deliberate intent of provoking this fight, with the deliberate intent of letting Wade whip him. It was a means, to Curt, of arousing sympathy for himself among the smaller ranchers. It was a means of arousing hostility toward the sheriff. And it undoubtedly had another purpose, too, that of planting the beginnings of a quarrel between Ellen and Wade. Neat. And effective. And Wade had stepped into it just as Curt had known he would.

Wade scowled and walked away from the crowd, heading across the street toward Prior's store. Sontag and another man were helping a half-conscious and muddy Curt McVey toward the saloon. A third man had picked up Curt's gun and was following while he wiped mud off it reverently with a bandanna.

Rain misted down and the sky was fast darkening with early dusk. Wade slogged through the mud, came up on the other side of the street, and angrily stamped mud from his boots on the walk. He went into Prior's.

It was a large, long building with a shed-roofed verandah across the front. The windows were loaded with an assortment of goods, ranging from rifles to bolts of cloth, from steel traps to carpenter tools. As he stepped into the door, the crowd that had been watching the fight made way for him. Prior was waiting on a man at the rear of the store.

Someone asked: "You give him his walking papers, Wade?"

Wade shook his head.

Another asked: "What was the fight about?"

Wade was silent, his face still and cold. The group shuffled their feet uneasily.

Prior, a short, colorless man with spectacles, finished with his customer, and Wade walked back to him. He said: "Can you get someone to replace my front window tonight, Wilbur?"

"I'll try." Prior's face was totally expressionless, yet Wade thought he detected a gleam of some well-concealed emotion in his shrewd eyes. Prior walked down the long aisle to the back room and Wade could hear him talking to someone there, probably to ageing Sime Oldbuck who was his store helper and also the town handy man. He came out smiling. "Sime says he'll get it in before dark."

"Thanks."

Wade walked out through the crowd, looking neither to right nor left. He crossed the street and went into the office, which was cold now from the air coming in through the broken window.

He sat down in his swivel chair and began to pack his pipe. He knew he had been a fool for hitting Curt. But he also knew he'd do it again under the same circumstances. He was going to marry Ellen and he'd not listen to that kind of talk from anyone.

But his thoughts did not relieve the depression that had troubled him ever since he'd first heard Curt was returning. There was trouble coming for all of Whitewater County, and it seemed he was powerless to avert it.

III

Ellen Santangelo stood, hands on hips, surveying the set table and frowning slightly. She could hear her father puttering with the stove in the parlor, building up the fire.

Ellen did not know, exactly, what it was that troubled her tonight. Hers was a mood of vague depression that seemed to be reasonless.

She whirled and returned quickly to the kitchen, to the steamy odor of frying steak, of baking rolls. Her father came out and pumped a wash basin full of water, then washed his hands.

Drying them, Mike Santangelo said: "There's talk around town that Curt McVey is coming back. Seems he spent last night at Rennick's."

Ellen froze, a piece of steak speared on a fork inches above the skillet. This, then, was the reason for her depression. Yet how had she known, how had she sensed that something was going to happen?

She was a small girl, dressed tonight in a gray and white gingham gown and wearing a bright red apron. Her copper-colored hair was gathered neatly in a bun on her neck, but tendrils of it had escaped and now framed her face that was slightly damp from heat and exertion.

She finished turning the steak, then brushed the tendrils of hair away from her forehead with the back of her wrist. She was conscious of her father's penetrating stare.

He said carefully: "Bother you some, honey, hearing about

Curt after all these years?"

She frowned. "Of course not," she said vehemently, perhaps too much so. She was silent for a few moments, and then asked: "What is he doing in Whitewater?"

Mike shrugged. He was a man of sixty, portly and genial. Mike had charge of the county roads and spent his days riding a road grader behind three teams of huge Percheron horses. Of Italian descent, his face had a swarthy color, deepened to mahogany from its constant exposure to sun and weather. "I don't know. Maybe he's just passing through." He sat down in a chair by the stove and busied himself with his curve-stemmed pipe.

"I hope so." The words escaped Ellen through no conscious will of her own.

"Why?" Mike looked at her penetratingly.

Ellen made an impatient gesture. "Dad, don't cross-examine me."

"Ain't you got over him yet?"

"Of course I have. Dad, stop this. Curt McVey is back in town. So he's back in town. Why should that affect me? Wade and I have our marriage plans made."

She opened the oven door and, stooping, drew out first one pan, and then another filled with golden brown, fragrant rolls. Her face, as she rose, was averted from her father's gaze.

It was a face no one would ever call pretty. Because it was beautiful. Her forehead, above her liquid brown eyes, was high and smooth. Her mouth was small, her cheeks slightly hollow beneath her high and rather prominent cheek bones. Her neck was a proud column that lost itself in the finely shaped hollows of her shoulders.

From the front of the house the doorbell jangled as someone gave it a vigorous twist, and Ellen said automatically: "Dad, go let Wade in."

She watched him go out of the kitchen, heard the door open, and heard Wade's voice and her father's talking. She put the rolls on a plate, the steaks on a platter, and carried them into the dining room, wondering what she would see on Wade's face. Would there be doubt there? Fear? Anxiety? Would he be as troubled by Curt's return as Ellen herself was? Or was he sure now, sure that nothing could come between them, could upset their plans?

She was thinking: *I was a fool! Wade is worth ten of Curt McVey.*

Wade had his back to her and was shrugging out of a wet sheepskin. When he turned, she saw the blue bruise on his left temple, the darkening right eye. His mouth was puffy and his lower lip was dark with a scabbed cut. He grinned at her and there was something sheepish in his grin.

Ellen felt a stir of unreasoning anger. Wade had been fighting with Curt McVey, that she knew immediately. He'd been fighting with Curt McVey, and Ellen knew the town would place but one possible interpretation on that.

She was definitely cool as she said: "Well, I see Curt is back."

Her father admonished: "Ellen, stop that."

She looked at him. "Why? Am I supposed to be glad because the man I am going to marry had a fight with one I used to know? Am I supposed to cheer because everyone in town is making sly jokes about it? Wade, I gave you credit for more sense than to fight with him."

There was a spark of anger in Wade's eyes. He said: "You're jumping to a conclusion. It happens you're right, but you didn't know you were."

"Did you order him out of town?" Ellen knew her dinner was getting cold, but a perverse anger kept her from caring. She knew, too, that she was likely to say things she'd be sorry for if she continued. She wanted to stop, yet she couldn't seem to manage it.

114

Wade shook his head. "No. I can't order him out of town."

"But you tried?"

"No." His eyes, looking at her so quietly, were puzzled. "What's the matter with you?"

"Nothing's the matter with me!" Her voice had risen. She knew she was very close to tears.

Her father repeated in an alarmed tone: "Ellen, stop it. Wade's done nothing so terrible."

She felt the tears beginning to sting beneath her eyelids, and that further angered her. She stamped a small foot. "Nothing so terrible? No, of course not. He's only had a public brawl with Curt. And there isn't a soul in Whitewater that doesn't know he hasn't anything particular against Curt except the fact that Curt and I used to go together. So they'll know the fight was over me. And every time I walk down the street, I'll see their sly smiles." She whirled on Wade. "I'd think you'd have had more respect for me than to let this happen! I'd think. . . ." The tears were flowing in earnest now, and a sob caught in her throat.

The worst of it was she knew she was being emotional, being a woman. She knew she would be sorry for this and yet she couldn't stop.

Angrily she whirled and rushed across the dining room to her bedroom door. She slammed the door behind her and turned the key in the lock.

Then, without lighting the lamp, she flung herself face downward on the bed and abandoned herself to her weeping.

She could hear, through the door, the muffled, deep sounds of the two men's voices. After a little while, she heard the front door open and close. Then silence, complete and profound.

She lay still for a long ten minutes, listening. Her mind, even while she listened, kept going back over the things she had said and she began to feel ashamed. Yet even while she was ashamed, she was remembering Curt, recalling his open, mocking grin, his wildness, his unruly, curly hair. She was remembering the strength of his arms and, flushing hotly there in the darkness, recalled the way she had felt every time he had kissed her.

She wondered: *Why did you have to come back, Curt? Why? And why did it have to be now? Why couldn't you have waited until Wade and I were married?*

She got up, went to the window, and stared outside. She was sorry now, as she had known she would be. She was sorry for the quarrel she'd made with Wade. Tomorrow she'd tell him she was sorry.

Or would she? Would she be able to swallow pride enough for that? Ellen shook her head, her cheeks wet with her tears, her eyes worried.

She crossed the dark bedroom and opened the door. The house was silent and she knew her father had left with Wade. Listlessly she began to pick up the dishes on the table, the untouched food that was now cold and unappetizing.

Ellen finished that, and sank into one of the straight-backed kitchen chairs. She held her hands clenched together in her lap. Her face was strained and pale.

Yes. She'd tell Wade she was sorry. And on the surface things would be as they'd been before. Yet down underneath both would know they weren't. Because both she and Wade would know that the shreds of Curt McVey's attraction remained, that neither of them could be happy until they had finally been dispelled.

Ellen could not remember ever having been quite so depressed as she was at this moment. And there was nothing she could do about it. Nothing at all.

Wade left the house with Mike Santangelo and the two walked in silence along the dripping street, their feet making sucking noises in the mud. They reached Main and paused in unspoken accord. Mike said: "The hotel?"

Wade shook his head. "You go ahead, Mike. I'm not hungry just now."

Mike gripped his arm companionably. "Can't say I blame you much." He stood there, still for a moment, his hand a strong, comforting pressure on Wade's arm. Cold rain misted down, lying in tiny, sparkling droplets on their coats, wetting their faces in spite of the protection of their wide-brimmed hats. At last Mike said reluctantly: "Run him out, Wade. Nobody will blame you even if it ain't quite legal."

Wade shook his head. He said: "Nobody ever whipped anything by running away from it, Mike. Ellen has got to find out, and I've got to find out, too."

Mike took his hand from Wade's arm. "She's a woman, Wade, and therefore not always reasonable."

"But it's not all gone, her feeling for him. If it had been, she'd never have blown up that way."

He could sense rather than see Mikes fatalistic shrug. "You're going to give up, then, rather than fight?"

Wade suddenly felt a stir of resentment, and a hard core of stubbornness within himself. He said coldly: "I don't want a woman that doesn't want me."

Mike regarded him thoughtfully. "Cool off, son. Cool off. I'll talk to you tomorrow."

Without giving Wade a chance to answer, he crossed the street, heading for the Great Western.

Wade watched him go, a shapeless, dimly seen figure in the poor light and misting rain. Meanness and jealousy ate at his brain. He wanted to hit something, to keep on hitting it. He wanted to hurt something.

He turned, hearing the mournful whistle of the 6:40 as it approached across the river valley, and walked slowly toward the station.

It was not Wade's custom to meet the train. He did it occasionally, however, when he'd nothing better to do. Tonight, he walked toward the depot because he didn't want to see anyone, because he didn't want to talk to anyone just yet. Later, perhaps, he could manage it. But not right now.

The platform was deserted. Through the lighted station window, Wade could see Rufus Horne, the station agent, poring over a pile of papers, his face all but invisible because of the green eye shade he wore on his forehead. At the edge of the platform the rails hummed with the train's approach.

The air was chilling rapidly. Wade judged that by morning, if it didn't stop, the rain would have turned to snow.

The train came in, steam hissing, brake shoes screaming. It slowed and pulled to a stop just beyond the station. The conductor hopped down and placed a step. Up in the doorway, Wade could see a woman's skirts.

The conductor helped her down, then tossed up the step, and walked over to the station for the mail sack. The woman, or girl as Wade saw now, stood hesitating in the rain, a small valise in her hand.

Wade walked toward her. She saw him, waited expectantly, but when she saw him reach into his shirt pocket for makings, something seemed to freeze in her. Wade realized that she had seen the star on his shirt front, and, if his earlier judgment of her had needed confirming, it was confirmed now. He faced her and shaped his smoke.

She was pale and young, and altogether devoid of make-up. But there was no mistaking her manner of dress, nor the peculiar wisdom in her eyes. Wade struck a match and touched it to the tip of his cigarette, cupping his hands against the wind.

She said in a low and husky voice: "Hello, Sheriff."

Wade nodded briefly, unsmiling.

She made a tired smile. "Going to tell me to get back on the train?"

He was surprised to discover himself shaking his head. "You can stay as long as you behave yourself. In Whitewater, only men are allowed in the saloons. There's no place for a girl like you."

It was a rather delicate situation, and Wade braced himself inwardly for her anger, for her bitter words. He was disappointed. She looked at him in a still-faced way for a moment, shrugged tiredly, and said: "Which way is the hotel?"

"I'll walk with you." He reached out and took her valise.

She gave it up reluctantly. "I'd rather you didn't."

"I'd do it for any woman who came in on the train. The street is muddy and the walks hard to find in the dark."

"All right, Sheriff. Thank you."

He turned, and she put out a small hand and took his arm. Together, unspeaking, they walked away from the platform and into the inky darkness. Wade led the way to the walk and guided her along it. He found himself feeling sorry for this girl, and wondering why she had come to Whitewater.

As they passed the Mesa Saloon, Wade heard a shout from inside. It was a boisterous, hilarious shout, and he recognized it immediately. His forehead furrowed with an irritated frown, for the shouting voice was easily recognizable as that of Curt McVey.

The girl halted abruptly, and Wade looked at her questioningly. She murmured: "He's here, then?"

"You know him?"

"Yes." She moved ahead and Wade walked with her. She did not elaborate upon her simple statement.

They came to the hotel and Wade pushed open the door for her, then came in after her.

He followed her across the tiled lobby that was thickly tracked with mud from the street. The clerk, a balding, paunchy man

119

looked up and made a knowing, bold smile. Wade stared him down harshly.

The girl said wearily: "A room, please."

The clerk looked questioningly at the sheriff, and Wade nodded almost imperceptibly. The clerk said—"Two-Oh-Four."—and gave her a key. She turned toward Wade and he handed her the valise. She made a smile that had no warmth and murmured: "Thank you, Sheriff."

"Sure." He stared at her as she crossed the lobby and climbed the stairs.

She was a small girl, no taller than Ellen. Even in her voluminous coat you could tell that she was slim and nicely made. But for her clothes, which told her calling so plainly, and the tired and ageless wisdom in her eyes, you might have mistaken her for just another weary and rather pretty girl. Wade turned away, thinking: *More trouble. More trouble because of that damned Curt McVey.*

He stalked angrily into the dining room.

IV

At 7:30, a man rode into Whitewater from the Cañon Creek road. There was something vaguely furtive about him, and, as he rode, his eyes kept darting back and forth, not because he anticipated trouble or danger, but simply because this was one of his ingrown habits.

The streets of Whitewater were deserted. Rain still came down drearily and steadily in a misty drizzle. It ran from the brim of the newcomer's hat in a slow stream whenever he tilted his head forward, but he seemed not to notice it.

Dim light filtered from the big windows of the Great Western Hotel, throwing a slight aura of illumination onto the verandah. Next door, the dirty windows of the Mesa Saloon glowed similarly. The sheriff's office, with its new window glass, was dark.

Gil Rennick dismounted before the saloon and made his tie at the rail. He paused on the walk for a moment as though trying to organize his thoughts.

Rennick was a small man, dressed in muddy Levi's and a ragged sheepskin coat from which the buttons were long since gone. A short piece of light rope was tied around his waist to hold the coat together, and he now fumbled at the knotted rope with his thin and bony hands.

His face was long and narrow, his nose and chin both pointed. He needed a shave badly, and from the appearance of him, he could have used a good washing, too.

He opened the saloon door and stepped inside. He finished untying the rope around his waist, wadded it up, and stuffed it into his coat pocket, throwing the coat open to the welcome heat of the room.

It was a smoky room, warm from the stove in its center, and smelling of cigars, man sweat, spilled whiskey, and wet wool.

There were perhaps a dozen men in the place, among them Sontag, over whom Rennick's close-set eyes brushed briefly, and Curt McVey. Rennick's glance found the latter and studied him carefully.

McVey's eyes were red and slightly fogged from drink. His lips were loose and slack. You could see something in Curt now that was not apparent in him sober. Something unpleasant. Something cruel and greedy. Rennick smiled almost imperceptibly.

McVey had apparently passed the hilarious stage of his drinking and was rapidly approaching another stage.

Rennick scratched his nose with a habitual, nervous gesture. He caught Sontag watching him, and, thumbing back his hat on his bald forehead, he approached the big Scandinavian. He

121

gestured with his head at Curt and asked: "You think he's too drunk? I had a hard time getting away. The blamed milk cows got into the alfalfa and I was afraid I'd lose 'em from bloat."

Sontag shrugged, saying in his deep voice: "We can find out."

Rennick looked at McVey again. So far, McVey appeared totally unaware of him. McVey was staring moodily at his drink, lost in his own gloomy thoughts. Rennick asked: "How'd he get beat up? Kellman?"

Sontag laughed shortly. His laugh was like the distant rumble of thunder. "Kellman never saw the day he could whip Curt. The sheriff done that."

"Wade? What for?"

Sontag shrugged again. "Ellen Santangelo likely. She used to be sweet on Curt. Maybe Wade's afraid Curt will take her away from him."

Rennick laughed. "He might, too. Go on over and see if he's too drunk to talk."

He watched as Sontag moved down the bar toward McVey. Sontag growled a few words in an undertone, and McVey looked up and met Rennick's eyes. Rennick grinned easily.

McVey nodded and came toward him with Sontag lumbering along behind. Rennick signaled the bartender, Shorty Drummond. He asked: "Card room empty, Shorty?"

Shorty nodded.

Rennick turned and led the way between the two pool tables in the rear of the saloon to the closed door of the card room. It was dark inside. He fumbled in his pocket for a match and lit the lamp on the table.

McVey came in behind him, and Sontag closed the door. Rennick sat down.

There was a certain sharpness in Rennick's eyes as he studied McVey, meanwhile gesturing toward a chair across the table from him. A certain shrewd sharpness, and a wary caution. He said: "We talked a little last night and I've been thinking about it since. You still interested? The sheriff hasn't changed your mind?"

Curt scowled. He said thickly: "I rigged that fight. I taunted him into it. And I let him beat me."

"Why?"

"Maybe because I want Ellen back."

"Wade doesn't intend to run you out of town, does he?"

Curt's face flushed darkly. "He never saw the day he could run me out of Whitewater. Get on with it. What the devil have you figured out?"

"We're going to take K Diamond." Rennick watched Curt's eyes widen, waited until he fully comprehended, and then went on. "They're big because we let 'em be big. The old man took part of my place and he took part of Sontag's Mill Iron before you killed him. We never got that back. We will now, and a lot more to go with it."

He heard Sontag make an uneasy growl. Curt looked interested but uncertain. Rennick let him digest this bold statement for a moment before he went on.

"This country owes you something, Curt, and now's your chance to get it. You throw in with Sontag and me, and you'll wind up with a damned good ranch."

"You can't take K Diamond."

Rennick laughed unpleasantly. "I can and I will. The only thing I can't take is a hundred and sixty acres. The part the house and buildings are on. But how big is K Diamond, Curt?"

"Ten, twelve, fifteen thousand acres maybe."

"And what title have they got to it?"

Curt was beginning to grin. "None. Prior usage is all. And they hold it."

"Then if we take it, it's ours. Right?"

"I guess so." Curt seemed confused by the enormity of the

proposal, and Rennick's lip curled almost imperceptibly. Curt said: "Wade Daugherty will never stand for it."

Rennick snorted. "He'll have to. There isn't one damned thing he can do about it. Kellman holds title to a hundred and sixty acres. And that's all. The rest is Public Domain. Like I said, Kellman is only big because we let him be big. But you're going to change that, Curt. Even if you have to kill him."

Curt's eyes had lost their confusion and he was rapidly getting rid of the effects of alcohol. He said: "And what part do I get out of it?"

Rennick settled back in his chair, relaxing now that he had Curt hooked. He said: "Write your own ticket. We split three ways and you get whichever part you want."

"Kellman will fight. At least Jesse will. And Sam'll do what Jesse says."

Rennick smiled slyly. "I'm counting on it. In fact, their fighting is part of the plan. But you'll be clear, Curt. I'll see that you're clear."

Curt looked at him with a certain distaste. Already, in the heat of the room, the unwashed smell of Rennick was beginning to fill the air. Curt said: "All right. You've got a man. When do we start?"

Rennick smiled at him patiently.

"What do you think I've been doing all day? We've already started."

From Whitewater, lying beside the White River, the land rose steeply, through tumbled fields of gigantic boulders, to the foot of the towering plateau. The plateau itself was cut and divided by numerous deep cañons, the main one of which carried the stream known as Cañon Creek.

These cañons, or valleys, varying from half a mile to five miles wide, were where the ranches lay. And of course, K

Diamond spread out across the Cañon Creek Valley and up it for almost fifteen miles.

According to the laws of the United States, K Diamond's bottom land was open for homesteading. In theory. In practice it was not. Ross Kellman had effectively discouraged a dozen attempts to settle it during his lifetime, and his sons had discouraged two or three since his death.

Above the bottom land, high on the top of the plateau, was the summer range of these valley ranches. And there, as in the bottom, K Diamond claimed and held the best, allowing the smaller ranchers to hold and use only the land on which the grass was poor, or on which there was inadequate stock water.

An old story. An oft-repeated one. Where land was free, the man with the most strength, the one unencumbered by conscience, would always own the best.

The morning after Curt McVey's arrival in Whitewater dawned clear and cold. The rain had changed to snow during the night and now an inch-deep layer of it lay upon the ground. The sagebrush, greasewood, and the locusts along the creek were covered thickly with its clinging whiteness, making a beauty that was almost indescribable against the intense blue of the sky.

Tony Lazzeri arose early, aware that much must be done today. For today was the day Gil Rennick had agreed to help him seize a branch of the Cañon Creek Valley for his own.

Tony was a short man, stocky and swarthy of skin. A peaceful man, who did his work, cared for his stock, and mostly avoided the company of his neighbors. He did not avoid them because he disliked them or because he disliked company. But only because he still had difficulty with the English language.

Tony had come to America only five years before. For a year he had worked in the coal mines of Pennsylvania, always dreaming of the time when he would have saved enough money to buy himself a small farm.

Free land had drawn Tony West as a magnet draws iron filings. He claimed 160 acres in a tributary of Cañon Creek, bought a few scrawny cows with the money he had been saving, and settled down to ranch.

He was not a greedy man. But he was a poor man, who over the years had acquired a deep-seated resentment of wealth. Also, he had learned to trust those of his kind, to whom hardship was commonplace, poverty expected. He therefore had trusted Gil Rennick yesterday when Rennick had come riding in and had told him the story of Curt McVey's return.

This morning, in pre-dawn gray, he fried himself a couple of pieces of venison steak and baked half a dozen biscuits. He ate the steak and biscuits and washed the meal down with half a pot of black, scalding coffee. When he was finished, he went outside.

Behind his single-room log cabin was a lean-to shed in which Tony kept his tools and supplies. He carried out a half dozen rolls of barbed wire, a bucket of staples, hammer, pliers, axe, shovel, and bar, and dumped them in a pile on the snowy ground. Then he went to the corral and caught a huge, shaggy black horse. He harnessed the horse and hitched him to a kind of sled called a stoneboat. On the stoneboat he piled his materials. Then he squatted, packed his pipe, and patiently waited.

The sun was just poking above the eastern rim of the plateau when he saw them coming. Two horsemen who he recognized at once as Gil Rennick and Curt McVey.

Tony had been here three years before when McVey had killed Ross Kellman. He had felt a vague sense of gratitude toward McVey then, for he had known Kellman intended seizing Tony's own land. Yet even then mixed with his gratitude was his instinctive abhorrence of McVey because he had killed.

The country called it a fair fight and the law did nothing. To

Tony, the killing was murder and would never be anything else, no matter how relieved he felt himself about Ross Kellman's death.

So it was with some trepidation, some timidity that he faced the pair this morning.

Rennick called, as soon as he came within hailing distance: "Ready, Tony?"

Tony nodded, smiling, watching McVey with uncertain eyes. There was a change in McVey that even Tony, who had scarcely known him before, could see. A change. A new hardness, a new callousness.

McVey grinned down at him. "Come along then," he said, and touched the grip of one of the holstered guns at his side. "I'll see to it that you get your fence strung without anybody bothering you."

Tony returned the grin, smothering his inward uneasiness. It was not likely that he'd be bothered while he was stringing the fence anyway. Kellman seldom got up this valley, at least until spring roundup started. It was unlikely he'd get up this way today.

Tony picked up the horse's lines and clucked him into motion. The stoneboat slid easily along the snowy ground. Rennick and McVey fell in behind.

Rennick said: "We'll string the fence across right at the mouth of the creek. That'll give you this whole damned valley, Tony. You can run three, four times as many cows as you run now. Anyhow, you got as much right to it as Kellman has."

Tony nodded, smiling. He did not reply. He was thinking that, with the whole valley, his cattle would be heavier, fatter when he shipped them each fall.

Rennick said: "We'll whip the Kellmans here in the valley before it's time to take the cattle out on top for the summer. You'll get your pick of the summer graze, too, Tony."

Tony felt a surge of gratitude. This Rennick, dirty and sly as he seemed, was a good friend. He had chosen to help Tony first, and Tony wanted to thank him for it.

He turned and glanced up at Rennick. He said haltingly in his broken English: "You're a good man, Mister Rennick. I will not forget."

Rennick flushed and looked at the ground. McVey was staring at the rim of the plateau. Tony returned his attention to his horse and stoneboat, understanding that they were embarrassed by his gratitude. *Good men,* he thought, *both of them.* Only different from himself.

At seven, they arrived at the mouth of the cañon and Rennick dismounted to help Tony.

Tony began at once, cutting cedar fence posts. Rennick used the horse, skidding them over and leaving them in a line that led upward from the creek toward the high and towering rims.

The plan was to throw a single wire across the valley to begin with. Later, more wires would be added until the fence was cattle-tight.

The morning wore on and the sun climbed slowly up the cloudless sky. McVey kept watch, lounging in his saddle, smoking cigarette after cigarette. Rennick, oddly, took great pains to keep his saddle horse near him at all times.

When Tony decided he had enough posts cut to last out the day, he stopped and walked over and began to dig post holes. Rennick, sweating in the sunlight, came behind him, setting the posts and tamping down the muddy ground around them with the bar.

The posts marched like sentinels from the creek toward the rim. But in mid-morning, Tony stopped, hearing McVey's call from below: "Look out! Here they come!"

Fear struck Tony instantly, fear that increased as Rennick, wordless, mounted his horse and galloped downslope to McVey.

After that, Tony saw the two ride into the heavy screening cover of willows and locusts along the creek and disappear.

His uneasiness increased sharply as the two Kellmans, Jesse and Sam, approached him, riding their horses at a walk up the steep slope.

A measure of confidence returned to Tony as he considered that very probably McVey and Rennick intended appearing at the crucial moment, intended coming up behind the Kellmans and surprising them.

Jesse Kellman was tall. Every year, Tony thought, he grew more like his father had been. His eyebrows were bushy and thick, his nose long and hooked. His eyes were as cold as bits of ice. He rode to within ten feet of Tony and said intemperately: "Just what the devil do you think you're doing?"

Tony could feel his face turn pale. He was a poor man, a little man, and he had never yet discovered the secret of faking assurance before the arrogance always shown him by men of power and wealth. He stammered a little, and finally got out haltingly: "I fence my valley. That is all."

"Your valley? *Your* valley?" Jesse Kellman's face grew red. The veins in his forehead swelled. He roared: "Damn you, this valley belongs to K Diamond. Always has. You got a little hundred and sixty acre claim at the upper end of it and that's all!" He turned to his brother. "Get busy, Sam."

Sam was as different from his brother as night from day. He was short, broad. His shoulders were tremendous and he had a chest like a beer keg. He made a wide, stupid grin with his thick-lipped mouth. His tiny eyes twinkled with dumb pleasure as he took down his rope.

For an instant, Tony Lazzeri knew raw fear. He shrank away. But apparently neither Jesse nor Sam intended physical violence today. Sam shook out his loop and dropped it over the nearest fence post. Dallying the rope around the saddle horn, he reined his horse around and jerked the post from the ground.

Jesse said: "Tony, take the rope off that post."

Tony looked toward the creek. Now was the time McVey and Rennick ought to be showing up. Yet he saw no sign of them. With surly reluctance he stooped and took Sam Kellman's loop off the post. Sam shook it out and roped the second post. Again he yanked it and again Jesse said: "The rope, Tony."

Slowly they worked downslope, with Sam yanking posts and Tony taking his loop off the post each time. Simmering, futile anger began to grow in Tony. But he was afraid to stop, for there was that in Jesse's eyes that warned him of the danger of stopping.

At length, they reached the floor of the valley and the last post was yanked. Sam coiled his muddy rope carefully and hung it from his saddle. Jesse sat, looking down at Tony. "You know what'll happen if you do this again?"

Tony shook his head fearfully.

Jesse scowled. "We'll put the rope on you, damn you. We'll drag you halfway to Whitewater." He turned to his brother. "Come on, Sam."

With never a backward glance, the two rode away.

Tony sat down on the stoneboat. He felt an overpowering weakness that was the reaction from sustained fear and anger over the past hour. That Rennick and McVey! His friends! They had ridden away like cowards, leaving Tony to face the Kellmans alone. Curse them! Curse them!

He did not know how long he sat there, but at last he heard a crashing of brush from the direction of the creek. He looked up, with a chill of fear shooting through him. Maybe the Kellmans had changed their minds. Maybe they had come back. . . .

But it was not the Kellmans who rode out of the willows. It was Rennick and McVey.

Tony stood up angrily. He shouted: "Curse you! You leave me

130

to face them alone!"

He could not understand the sudden coldness that formed in his belly. Rennick and McVey came on, riding side-by-side, and in them both was the oddest kind of tension. Rennick's face was utterly lacking in color and his eyes would not meet Tony's. McVey seemed overly nervous and he kept licking his lips.

Rennick said in a high, thin voice: "All right, Curt."

Curt's hand went to the gun at his side. It came out of the holster and leveled briefly.

Shock ran through Tony. His mouth came open and his cry bubbled out: "No! What are you doing?"

The *click* of Curt's gun hammer coming back was loud and clear in the still air. His horse fidgeted, but the gun stayed lined on Tony's chest.

Tony stood frozen, unable to move. Smoke puffed from the gun's muzzle. Something struck Tony in the chest and drove him back violently. He heard the roaring report of the gun. He felt briefly the cold mud and snow into which he fell.

Then the light faded slowly from the sky and he was falling, falling into a bottomless pit. And Tony Lazzeri was dead.

With shaking hands, Curt ejected the spent cartridge from his gun. He tossed it over toward where the milling tracks of the Kellmans' horses were. He took a fresh cartridge from his belt and shoved it into the empty cylinder chamber. Then he holstered the gun. He looked at Rennick. "I didn't like that. I never killed a man like that before."

Rennick's face was gray. He cleared his throat nervously. "I didn't like it, either. But, damn it, can't you see it was necessary?"

McVey turned his horse without answering.

Rennick followed. When they had gone perhaps a mile, he called: "Tear off a piece of your shirt tail and clean your gun!

Go down to the creek and wash your hands. Then we'll go in and see the sheriff."

V

Wade Daugherty got back to town at noon, tired from trying to patch up a quarrel between a man and his wife who lived about three miles downriver. The woman had driven into town in mid-morning with one of her eyes black. Her husband, she said, was drinking, and she feared for her own safety and that of the children.

Wade had ridden out behind her buckboard and had spent the rest of the morning listening to the sordid details of a family quarrel, coming away only half satisfied with the way he had patched it up.

It was this part of being sheriff that he disliked, this being forced to become a part of things that should have remained private.

He took his dinner in the hotel dining room and afterward bought a cigar at the desk and idly stood in the lobby while he bit off one end and stuck it between his teeth.

Standing there, he heard a woman's soft voice at the desk behind him. "Has Mister McVey come in yet?"

"No, ma'am. He went out about daylight and he hasn't come back." The clerk managed to get into his voice a certain bold insolence that did not escape Wade.

Wade turned and saw the girl he had escorted from the railroad station last night.

He smiled as he caught her eye and she walked toward him. "I wanted to see Curt. Do you have any idea . . . ?"

Wade shook his head. The top of the girl's head came just to his throat. Her hair was brown, and smooth like silk. Her eyes were worried and her face pale. Wade said: "He'll be back."

"Yes. Yes, of course he will. Thank you." She made a weak

132

smile and crossed the lobby to the dining room. Wade noticed that she was dressed more simply today, more conservatively, and he liked the change.

He strolled out to the verandah and paused to light his cigar. The sun shone brightly down into the muddy street. Light green showed on the town's lawns where last night's snow had melted.

Wade felt an odd depression. He was worried, for one thing, about Ellen, and debating whether he should not walk over to her house and talk to her. Yet the quarrel had been of Ellen's making, and he hesitated because he was not sure she was ready to make up. Or even that she wanted to.

Shrugging lightly, he picked his way across the street and went into his office. There was an odd smell here that he always noticed when coming in from outside. It was the smell of disinfectant used in the jail behind the office. Acrid and faint, it was a smell Wade had never encountered anywhere else.

He sat down at his desk, frowning, wondering now where Curt McVey was, what he was doing.

He came to his feet as the door opened and Ellen Santangelo came in. She was smiling hesitantly, flushed lightly. Her eyes met his directly. She said at once: "Wade, I'm a little beast, aren't I?"

He grinned. "No, I don't think so. I like you."

"Last night was terrible. I'm so ashamed of myself."

He crossed the office to her. His mood of depression was gone, and he felt a stir of affection for her. And pride because she could be so direct about this. He put his arms around her waist. "Forget it. It's all over. But you owe me a steak dinner."

"I'll have it tonight. And apple pie. All right?"

He pulled her to him roughly and kissed her thoroughly. For just an instant she kissed him back, but then she began to struggle and he let her go. She said with embarrassment: "Wade, not here! Not in the sheriff's office."

133

"Where would you suggest?" he teased.

He liked the way her color heightened even as her eyes met his. And suddenly they were both laughing, the quarrel was forgotten, and the day was good. Ellen turned toward the door. "I'll see you tonight, then. Am I forgiven?"

"Sure. Sure you are." He watched her go out and cross the street toward Prior's store.

Standing at the window, staring out, he saw the two horsemen that swung at a gallop off the Cañon Creek road and into Main, recognizing them immediately. He heard a shout, this coming from Rennick, but could not distinguish the words. Yet he saw the way action suspended in the people on the street, the way they stared. That and the expressions on both riders' faces told him instantly that the trouble had begun.

He went to the door and yanked it open just as Rennick and McVey drew their horses to a plunging halt before the office. Rennick yelled in his thin, high voice: "They got Tony! Wade, they got Tony!"

"Tony? What the devil are you talking about? Who got Tony?"

"The Kellmans did. Jesse an' Sam." Rennick piled off his horse, muddy, unshaven as usual. He stood on the walk holding the trembling, sweaty horse's reins. The horse stamped nervously.

Wade said: "Easy now. Get your breath, and then tell me what happened."

McVey still sat his horse in the street, looking down, with no smile softening the line of his mouth. His eyes did not meet Wade's.

Rennick babbled: "We was helping Tony string fence across the Deep Creek Valley. . . ."

Wade interrupted: "That's K Diamond range."

Rennick said defiantly: "It's open range. It's Public Domain."

Wade shrugged. "Go on."

Rennick said: "Tony an' me was working up on the hillside, setting posts. The Kellmans rode up an' started raising hell. They yanked out all the posts we'd set. When we all got down by the creek, Jesse pulled out his gun an' killed Tony. Then they all rode away."

"Where was Curt all this time?" He looked at Curt suspiciously.

Rennick said hastily: "Tony sent Curt back to his shack for some wire stretchers. Curt didn't get back until the Kellmans had gone."

A crowd was forming now, gathering in a semicircle behind the sheriff. He turned, saw the stableman, Russ Fagin, among them. He said: "How about a buckboard and team, Russ?"

"Sure. Right away."

"And a saddle horse. My gray will do."

"Sure." Russ hurried away.

Wade said: "I want a couple of men to drive up and get Tony's body."

There was an instantaneous murmur of voices as half a dozen men volunteered. Wade picked two of them and sent them to the stable for the buckboard that Russ was hitching up. Then he waited.

Ellen Santangelo came out of Prior's with a couple of older women and the three stood there, looking across the street. Curt noticed Ellen and looked at Wade. "You want me for anything?"

Wade shook his head. Curt rode across the street and dismounted before Prior's store. He looped his reins around the rail and stepped up onto the verandah, facing Ellen and removing his hat.

Wade, watching Ellen, saw her nervous smile. He wished he were closer so that he could tell exactly what expression her face held at this first meeting with Curt in three years. He scowled and looked away.

Russ Fagin came riding up the street mounted on Wade's gray gelding and dismounted. He handed the reins to Wade. Wade wanted to look across the street at Ellen and Curt, but he was hanged if he'd give the watching townspeople that much satisfaction.

But as he swung into his saddle, he did manage to steal a quick glance that way. Curt was smiling, standing close to El-len. And Wade could have sworn that Ellen's eyes were sparkling as she moved on down the boardwalk with the two women.

That glimpse of Ellen, and Curt's assurance, caused a sud-den, sour violence to come to Wade's thoughts. Hang it, how much was a man supposed to stand without blowing up? He experienced a return of the feeling he'd had last night, that vi-cious desire to strike out, to hurt something. Knowing he ought to control it, he nevertheless was human enough, perversely, not to want to at all.

Rennick caught his glance as he wheeled away. Had Rennick been wise enough to hold his face expressionless in that briefest of instants, all might have been well. But apparently Rennick could not resist showing Wade a triumphant, mockingly smug grin. And Wade could not resist reining his horse against Ren-nick.

He reached down as he did and caught Rennick by the front of his shirt. "You damned little weasel! What are you smirking about? Tony Lazzeri's dead. Is that funny?"

The mocking humor faded from Rennick's sharp face with the contact, to be replaced at once by a wild, raw anger. Ren-nick choked: "Damn you! Let me go."

"Yeah. When I'm ready. You masterminded all this business, didn't you, Gil? Curt stopped at your place on the way into town. He stayed the night. You had a lot of time to talk to him. You planned all this. The pair of you went up there and talked

Tony into grabbing a chunk of K Diamond, and, when the Kell-mans showed up, you and Curt disappeared."

Rennick's expression closed down, became blank and cautious. But the anger remained, making his close-set eyes glitter, making his thin mouth a narrow gray line. Rennick said: "Turn me loose, damn you, or you'll be. . . ."

"I'll be sorry?" Wade laughed harshly. He tightened his grip on Rennick's shirt front until the little man was choking for breath. He said: "Don't get too greedy too fast, little man. K Diamond's a big cheese. You can't gobble it up in a day, even with Curt to help you."

Rennick was small, but his muscles were wire and he was fast as light. He opened his mouth, cursed Wade obscenely, and found a snap-blade knife somewhere in his pockets and slashed at Wade's leg.

But Wade saw this coming and flung Rennick from him with an expression of disgust.

The knife, slashing so wildly, missed Wade's leg, but it inflicted a deep cut on the hip of Wade's horse. The animal snorted, lunged away, and reared.

Wade leaped clear, his temper at last running wild. He growled: "Why, you scrawny son-of-a-bitch!"

For reply, Rennick laughed. His tiny eyes were bright; his mouth was tight with rat-like courage. He snarled: "Big man, ain't you, Sheriff? Come on, I'll whittle you down to size."

A voice somewhere yelled: "Hey! Rennick's been eating raw meat!"

Rennick came darting in, the knife slashing expertly, all restraint gone. Wade leaped back, but he felt the heat of the knife tip as it tore through his sleeve and drew blood from his arm.

And Wade knew a bleak self-disgust. For the second time in as many days he had let his temper suck him into a stupid, losing fight. First with Curt, now with Rennick. Win, lose, or draw, the fight would react inevitably to Wade's disadvantage. A sheriff ought to use more judgment.

Yet he knew that now he could not walk away. Neither could he use his gun. It was bare hands against Rennick's knife, poor odds at best.

Rennick came in again, for all the world like a weasel attacking a wolf. It was slash and leap away, jab and retreat. And again Wade felt the bite of that knife, this time a pricking of his chest.

Rennick was insane with a savage kind of courage, which was puzzling to Wade, who had never before seen this side of him. What had provoked it to come out of its hiding place behind Rennick's sly amiability? What stress had brought it forth?

One thing might have brought it out—a foretaste of power. Wade was suddenly sure that Rennick was behind all the trouble—that his accusations and suspicions about Rennick had been right. Very probably Rennick, and not the Kellmans, was behind Tony Lazzeri's death.

All of which was driven from his mind instantaneously by Rennick's renewed and savage attack. Rennick leaped in and his knife ripped Wade's coat from shoulder to waist. And Wade knew the cold touch of fear. If he were unable to catch Rennick's knife wrist—and soon. . . .

He crouched, turning constantly to face the dancing Rennick. Rennick's face was flushed, sweating, insane. He mouthed the words: "I'll kill you! I'll cut you to bits!"

Wade could hear someone's harsh and rapid breathing and realized it was his own. Fool! Fool for letting himself be drawn into this. Fool for letting jealousy turn into temper.

Rennick darted at him, knife hand flashing. This time Wade made a desperate grab for the knife. His hand closed on its blade and tightened down. He felt the bite of knife into flesh, but he did not let go. Groping with his other hand, he felt vast relief as it closed on Rennick's right wrist.

He released the knife, his hand dripping blood. He twisted with his other hand until Rennick shrieked with pain, and dropped the knife.

Rennick was almost sobbing, so desperate was his fight for breath, so vast was his frustrated rage. With a gesture of revulsion, Wade again flung the little man from him. Rennick dived for the knife, but Wade lunged forward and put his foot on it, leaving Rennick on his knees, groping in the mud.

Wade said, feeling almost physically sick: "All right, go on home, Rennick. Go home and cool off."

Someone in the crowd asked incredulously: "Hell, ain't you going to throw him in jail? Are you nuts, Wade?"

Wade realized that his aggravation of Rennick had either not been seen or had been interpreted wrongly. He realized that so far as the onlookers were concerned, he was clear of blame for this fight with Rennick. But his innate honesty would not let him thus easily avoid blame, which in part at least was his. He looked at the questioner, shaking his head. He said: "No. No jail. I started it."

Rennick got to his feet. His eyes held a murderous hatred as they stared at Wade. But they were puzzled, too, as though his sly and devious mind simply could not credit what Wade had done.

Wade caught his horse and mounted, giving the cut a superficial examination and deciding it was not too serious. For an instant he sat looking down at Rennick. He fumbled a bandanna from his pocket and wrapped it around his cut hand before he spoke. He repeated: "All right, get going."

For reply, Rennick cursed him.

VI

Wade frowned, touched spurs to the gray's sides, and cantered up the muddy street without looking back.

He was realizing that Curt had not disappointed him. He had expected Curt to stir up trouble and Curt had done so promptly. For without Curt's presence to back them up, neither Rennick nor Tony Lazzeri would have had the nerve to try running a fence across Deer Creek Cañon.

Now Tony was dead. And Tony was only the beginning. Tony was only a pawn that Rennick had been willing to sacrifice to involve the Kellmans with the law.

The sun beat down warmly on Wade's back as he rode. Light steam rose from the road and from the ground out on the sagebrush flats. A darting bit of blue settled on a greasewood branch and Wade saw that it was a bluebird, the first he'd seen this year.

Spring was coming, and with its coming the trouble would intensify. Wade rode steadily, pushing his horse, and at last came to the mouth of Deer Creek.

He made a wide pass across the valley, studying the ground. He picked up Rennick's and Curt's tracks going in and coming out. Farther on, he picked up the tracks of the Kellmans.

The first set he noticed was going in, and obviously the Kellmans had been in a hurry, running their horses. A light frown touched Wade's forehead, a frown that deepened a little farther on where he crossed the second set of tracks made by the Kellmans. These had been made by horses at a leisurely walk.

For a moment Wade sat still in his saddle, holding his horse quiet, staring down at the tracks. Something was wrong. If a man had just finished shooting down another in cold blood, if he knew that somewhere close by was Curt McVey, he would not be leisurely about leaving.

Puzzled, Wade rode along, backtracking here, and came at

last to Tony Lazzeri's crumpled body where it lay on the muddy ground.

He halted his horse about ten yards from the body, still studying the ground. His eyes picked up a glint of brass and he stepped from his saddle, walked over, and picked up a .44 brass cartridge case.

Prints here were blurry and indistinct, for this spot had apparently been shaded from the sun by the high rim until after the prints had been made. As soon as the sun had struck here, then the mud had softened and blurred the prints.

Still unsatisfied, Wade kept circling. But he found nothing more of use to him. There were several sets of tracks leading from this spot toward Tony's shack, but they were all unidentifiable because of the softening mud.

Wade returned to the scene of the crime. Tony was unarmed, so that made it a clear-cut case of murder. He dismounted, unharnessed the work horse from the stoneboat, and turned him loose. He piled the harness on top of the stoneboat. By the time he had finished, he could hear the rattling of the approaching buckboard.

He stayed long enough to help the two men lift Tony's body into it. Then he rode away again, heading this time toward Kellmans' K Diamond spread.

There were two horses standing tied beside the big log house. Two horses with muddy legs and sweaty hides. Wade swung stiffly down and walked to the back door. It opened as he reached it and Jesse Kellman stood framed in the doorway.

Kellman was scowling. "I was coming in to see you this evening."

"To give yourself up?"

Kellman's eyes widened, then narrowed with sudden anger. "Talk sense, Wade. What the devil would I give myself up for?"

"Killing Tony Lazzeri." Wade's eyes were cold, watchful. But there was puzzlement growing within him, too. This Kellman was either innocent of that or a damned good actor.

Jesse Kellman's face grew red. "Come on in, Wade. By Judas, there's something here that needs straightening out. So Tony's dead, is he?"

He stepped back away from the door, and Wade went in. Sam Kellman sat at the kitchen table, a cup of steaming coffee before him. He looked up at Wade with almost bovine puzzlement. Wade pulled out a chair and straddled it, resting his arms on its back. Jesse nodded to the cook, an unshaven oldster, who set a cup before Wade and poured it full.

Wade said wearily: "Tony's dead with a bullet in his heart. Let's see your gun, Jess. Yours, too, Sam."

Reluctantly Jesse withdrew his gun from its holster and laid it on the table. Wade said: "Forty-Four, ain't it?"

Jesse nodded. Wade picked up the gun, checked the loads, and smelled the barrel. "When'd you fire it last?"

"This morning. At a coyote out by the corral."

Wade nodded cryptically. "Get him?"

"No." Jesse was getting nervous.

Wade picked up Sam's gun, a nickel-plated Colt Lightning in a .38 caliber. He laid it back down again and fished the empty cartridge from his pocket. He laid it on the table. "I found this near Tony's body."

Jesse picked it up. The color faded from his face.

Wade said: "You rode up Deer Creek and found Tony and Rennick fencing. You. . . ."

Jesse interrupted intemperately: "Damn it, Wade, this is all wrong. Tony was alone. Sam yanked the posts with his rope, and, when we got that done, I told Tony that if he tried it again, I'd put the rope on him and drag him halfway to Whitewater. He was alive when we left."

"You didn't see Rennick or Curt McVey?"

"Hell no! Were they around? By Judas, I might have known."

Wade murmured wearily: "I've got to take you in, Jesse."

"Like the devil you will!" Jesse grabbed for the gun on the table. But Wade's gun was out of the holster and in his hand. The hammer coming back made a loudly audible *click*. He cautioned: "I wouldn't, Jesse."

He seemed almost negligent, but there was that in his eyes that apparently told Jesse he wasn't. Sam sipped his coffee, unmoving. With his left hand, Wade picked up the Lightning and tossed it under the stove, sliding. The .44 he stuffed in his belt.

He said: "Jesse, maybe you did it and maybe you didn't. But the fact is you were up there. You had a quarrel with Tony. Your gun's been fired and I found a Forty-Four cartridge beside the body. Rennick says he saw you pull the trigger. And lastly, Tony was unarmed." He looked at Jesse Kellman calmly. "I'm the sheriff. Could I do anything but take you in?"

"But I didn't do it!" There was growing desperation in Jesse's voice. "That damned Rennick is lying. He knows that if you put me in the clink, then he and the rest of the small cowmen can move in on K Diamond with no one to stop them."

"Sam'll be here."

Jesse laughed harshly. "Yeah. Sam'll be here." He shrugged and reached for his sheepskin that was hanging on a nail. Wade watched him closely.

Sam looked up stupidly and said: "You goin' to let him take you, Jess?"

Wade picked up the coffee cup and sipped it without taking his eyes from Jesse.

Jesse nodded at his brother shortly. "Look after things, Sam. I'll be back in a few days." He turned to Wade. "All right, damn it. Let's go. But I want a coroner's inquest on it tomorrow. So I can get back home."

Wade stood up. He followed Jesse out the door, watched the man mount, then mounted himself, cognizant both of Jesse and of the back door. The two rode out without incident.

Wade was beginning to feel doubtful, beginning to wonder if he were not playing into Rennick's and McVey's hands by arresting Jesse Kellman. He was beginning to believe that all this was just too pat.

If he'd ever seen a convincing demonstration of innocence, he'd seen it this afternoon in Jesse Kellman. With his forehead furrowed by a doubtful frown, he followed Jesse down the road toward Whitewater.

The mood of the town was hostile as Wade rode into its limits with Kellman, and Wade judged that Tony Lazzeri's body had arrived. There was a crowd of men down in front of Prior's and all along the street were small groups, talking. Wade and Kellman were targets for every eye on Main Street.

In the group before Prior's, Wade spotted McVey, Rennick, and Sontag, along with half a dozen of the other smaller ranchers.

He drew up before the sheriff's office and, without dismounting, watched Kellman climb down. Then he swung himself down and followed Kellman in.

Kellman hesitated before the door that led back to the jail cells. Wade waited patiently and with understanding until he had overcome his reluctance.

Kellman was scowling and pale as he walked into one of the cells. Wade closed the door and locked it behind him.

Kellman growled: "This is a devil of a thing. Dammit, how much chance do you think I've got, locked up here? I didn't kill Tony, but who'll believe that? They hate K Diamond and this will make a good chance for all of them to get even."

Wade said gravely: "No one will get even with you while

you're in my custody."

Kellman made a sour grin. "I wasn't thinking of a lynch party. I was thinking about K Diamond. Rennick and McVey put Tony up to fencing off Deer Creek. How long do you think it will be before they start grabbing the rest? Judas, Wade, K Diamond only holds a hundred and sixty acres by deed. We hold the rest by prior usage and force. With me in jail and the country against us how long do you think we can hold on?"

Wade said: "Not long."

Kellman said with quiet desperation: "Then do something!"

Kellman was a big, tall, raw-boned man, with not much flesh on his bones. His face was craggy, generous, and arrogant. His eyes were sharp and cold. He'd grown up under old Ross Kellman's thumb, and after Ross's death hadn't had much time for anything but running K Diamond, a task he'd had to learn almost from scratch since old Ross hadn't taken anyone into his confidence while he was alive. Wade doubted if Jesse had even seen the ranch books until after the old man was killed.

To his credit was the fact that he hadn't continued old Ross's greedy policy of grabbing range from his neighbors, and this should have built good will for K Diamond among their smaller neighbors. Strangely enough, it hadn't, and all they remembered now was the injury they had suffered at old Ross's hands.

Wade said: "There's nothing I can do. I'm sheriff and you're a murder suspect."

Kellman looked at him bitterly. "You're one of them. You're in with them."

Wade shook his head patiently. "You know better than that, Jess."

"Then try to see my side of it. You've got nothing but the most circumstantial kind of evidence to hold me on. Sure, I saw Tony. I was mad, too. Sam yanked his blamed fence posts and I made Tony help him. I threatened him, but not with killing. I

145

threatened to drag him at the end of a rope if he tried it again. And that was as far as it went. I swear that's the truth, Wade. Don't you believe me?"

Wade said wearily: "Jess, darn it, it isn't what I believe or what I don't. It's what the court will believe."

"Sure. Sure. Ease out of it that way. But the responsibility for what happens is on your shoulders, Wade, no matter how you try to talk yourself out of it."

Kellman walked over and sat down on the plank bench. He stared without hope at the cell floor.

Wade said: "All right. Someone killed Tony. If it wasn't you, then who was it?"

"Rennick or McVey, probably. Rennick's a crummy, sly little son-of-a-bitch. And McVey's a killer."

"But why would they . . . ?" Wade stopped, for he knew the answer.

Kellman looked at him, saw that he did, but filled in for him anyway: "They wanted me in jail. It serves a double purpose for them. For one thing, it puts the country solidly on their side of this. Everybody hates the Kellmans and K Diamond to one degree or another. This justifies their hatred." He got up, paced to the bars, and gripped them with his big, bony hands so hard the knuckles turned white. "The other reason is obvious. With me out of the way, there won't be much resistance to their grabbing K Diamond. Sam will try, but he's not very bright. He'll probably go barging around like a mad bull until he runs into someone's bullet. And they'll make it stick. In a week's time, they'll have K Diamond."

"Maybe you'll get out in a week. What will you do then?"

Kellman's eyes blazed. "I'll take back every damned acre they've stolen. I'll take it back if I have to kill every trespasser I find."

"You think they'll give it up?"

Kellman's mouth thinned. "Dead men can't hold land."

The light that came through the small cell windows was fading, was rapidly turning gray. Wade shrugged dispiritedly and walked into the office. He lit a lamp, brought it back into the cell-block, and set it up on a shelf provided for that purpose. He looked over at Kellman and said: "Anything special you want for dinner?"

Kellman shook his head without looking up.

VII

Wade closed the door and went into the office. He took time to pack a pipe and light it. Then he went out into the street, closed and locked the door behind him.

Most of the street crowd had dispersed, for the excitement was over now. Rennick and McVey and the smaller cowmen had probably gone into the Mesa Saloon.

Wade crossed the street, passed Prior's store, and paused before the building next door. This was the undertaking establishment that Prior ran in conjunction with his store.

Wade tried the door and found it open.

He went inside and closed the door behind him. A smell of new pine lumber came to him from the rear of the room. It was back there that Sime Oldbuck built caskets, and he'd probably been building one this afternoon.

The room was almost completely bare of furniture. In its exact center was a long, oak table. Tony's body lay on the table, covered by a sheet.

Along the walls were perhaps eight or ten straight-backed chairs.

There was a hanging lamp over the table. Wade walked over to it, raised the chimney, and touched a match to its wick. He lowered the chimney and looked down at Tony's body. He peeled back the sheet.

Tony's face, so swarthy and dark in life, was now waxen. He seemed smaller than Wade remembered him. There was a bloodstain on the front of his shirt as big as Wade's hand.

The door opened behind Wade, and Wade turned. Doc Sayers came shuffling in. He closed the door carefully behind him and advanced toward Wade, swaying slightly as he walked. He said: "The first of many, Sheriff. Looks like the county coroner is going to have to go to work for a change."

Wade said: "That's a bad joke, Doc."

Doc peered at him with his vague, pale eyes. He said: "It's no joke, Sheriff. There'll be more of these. Unless you keep Jesse Kellman locked up."

"I'm not so blamed sure Jesse killed him."

Doc was bending over Tony's body. He seemed to have lost interest in Wade. He said musingly: "Life is a wonderful thing. But when it's gone, there's nothing left, is there?"

Wade felt strangely uneasy. "This is the first time you've looked at him?"

Doc nodded without taking his glance from Tony. And Wade noticed for the first time the black bag in Doc's hand. He said: "I'd like to see the bullet. Think you could find it?"

Doc set his bag on the table. "Sure. Won't take a minute."

Wade turned his back and walked to the window. In the street a man passed and stopped to stare curiously inside. Angrily Wade jerked down the shades. He waited, knowing what Doc was doing behind him, and turned uneasy by the knowledge.

At last Doc grunted with satisfaction. Wade didn't turn and Doc came over and handed him a small piece of lead. Doc said: "Forty-Four."

"Yeah. It would be." Wade looked at the bullet, then dropped it into his pocket. He asked: "Doc, if you held an inquest tomorrow, what would your verdict be?"

"Why, Sheriff, you know that. I'd name Jesse Kellman."

Wade stared at him thoughtfully for a moment. "I thought so."

Doc asked defensively: "What other verdict could there be?"

Wade smiled. "None on the evidence you've got. Well, good night, Doc." He turned and went to the door, troubled vaguely.

In the street, he faced his thoughts squarely, and realized at last that he himself did not think Kellman guilty. It was all too pat. Firstly, Jesse and Sam Kellman had ridden into the mouth of Deer Creek valley at a lope, and come out at a walk. Secondly, they had made no attempt to hide their trail or to deny that they'd been there and seen Tony. Jesse had even admitted openly the fact that he'd quarreled with Tony over the fencing of Deer Creek Valley.

Yet if Jesse had not killed Tony, then Rennick was lying. And if Rennick was lying, it meant he knew who had really killed Tony.

Wade had had, in the years he'd been sheriff, some considerable experience with lawbreakers. Yet in all that time, he'd never yet found one who could kill in cold blood a man against whom he had nothing personal, for a motive that had nothing whatever to do with the victim.

It passed belief in his mind that anyone could be so totally cold-blooded. Yet what else could he think?

A light, cool wind blew down Cañon Creek, a wind fragrant with the smell of thawing earth and wood smoke. A gust of it brought to Wade the smell of food cooking in the hotel kitchen, and he remembered that he was expected at Ellen's for supper.

He hated to face her, and the very thought of her further complicated his problem. If Rennick had lied about Tony's death, then the logical assumption was that Curt McVey was probably the guilty man. And the minute Wade moved against McVey, he would lay himself wide open to charges of persecution. Ellen would believe he accused Curt from motives of jealousy. And the town would share her belief.

He shook his head violently as though to clear away his troubled thoughts. Then briskly he walked to the hotel and put in his order for Kellman's supper tray.

When it was ready, he carried it across the street and into the jail. He unlocked the cell door and took it inside, setting it down on the rough plank table.

Jesse Kellman looked up at him with smoldering eyes. He said: "Do you know that this is the first time in my life I've been in jail?"

Wade said: "Jess, did you see anything at all of Rennick or McVey up there where Tony was fencing?"

Jesse shook his head. He looked at Wade helplessly, and gradually a new light came into his eyes. He said: "Wade, if you killed a man in cold blood, with another watching, would you ride off and leave that witness there to testify against you?"

Wade started to shake his head, then hesitated. "I might, if I figured I had him scared enough."

Kellman's shoulders seemed to sag.

Wade said: "Eat your dinner, Jess. I'll be back later."

He went out into the street, carefully locking the door behind him. Across the street, he saw the girl he had escorted from the railroad station last night come out of the hotel. She walked purposefully to the Mesa Saloon and paused uncertainly there before it. Then, as though having made up her mind, she opened the door and went inside. Wade turned and headed for Ellen's house.

Ginny Martin felt a genuine fright as she stepped into the Mesa Saloon. It was not that she was unfamiliar with saloons, for she was not. She had worked in a number of them, as piano player and as singer.

But now she stood just inside the door, white-faced, silent, afraid. A man staggered away from the bar, approached the door, and stopped to peer owlishly at her. He grinned. "Well, now, look who's here!"

Ginny smiled weakly. The man reached for her, but she evaded him nimbly. He fell.

The sound of his falling attracted the attention of the men at the bar, among them Curt McVey. The impact of his eyes upon Ginny was almost physical. But he came to her at once.

"What are you doing here?"

Before she could answer, the drunk staggered to his feet, still reaching out for her. Curt stepped between the man and Ginny, and the man cursed. He turned and stumbled out of the saloon.

Curt repeated: "What are you doing here?"

Ginny shook her head. There was a strangeness about Curt that confused her. She murmured: "Isn't there somewhere we can talk? Come outside and walk with me."

He frowned. "I'm busy." He looked at her a moment more, finally saying irritably: "Well, all right."

Ginny went out, and Curt followed close behind. He walked north toward the edge of town with Ginny beside him. She reached out to take his arm, but he pulled it out of her reach.

She said: "Something's the matter. Perhaps I should get on the next train and go back."

Curt shrugged.

Ginny wished she could see his face, but it was only a pale shadow in the darkness. Ginny began to feel a vague, resentful anger. She said: "Curt, you asked me to marry you! That's why I came . . . why I followed you. I was afraid for you. I was worried. Is that so wrong?"

He said: "I told you I'd come back . . . or send for you. Why couldn't you leave it at that?"

"Perhaps I should have." She struggled with her pride, and finally overcame it. She asked: "Why did you come here, Curt?

Why? Already there's been a killing. And from the talk I've heard, it is only the beginning."

They had reached the spot where the boardwalk ended. Beyond stretched a muddy path. Ginny stopped. She turned toward Curt, waiting. She was surprised at his coldness and afraid because of it.

He began to talk, slowly at first but with increasing rapidity. "Ginny, I was raised in Whitewater County. It's home to me. Maybe that's why I came back."

"There's more to it than that."

"Sure. Sure there is. A devil of a lot more. We lived on a little homestead claim up Cañon Creek and K Diamond was all around us. There was always pressure on my old man. Pressure to get the devil out and leave the homestead go back to Public Domain. Fences would get torn down and cattle would get into the crops. Other things happened, like a work horse getting shot accidentally during hunting season. Accidentally, hell! None of it was accidental. We came home from town one time when I was about fourteen and found the cabin burned to the ground." He was tense and still for a moment. "My old man quit that night. We packed up what there was and left the country. Went down to Moab. I had a lot of kid ideas about getting even. I started to learn about guns. When I was twenty, the old man died. I sold out what little stuff the old man had and came back to Whitewater. I hung around two, three years. Then Kellman began pressuring the little cowmen again. He grabbed a slice of Sontag's place and a chunk of Rennick's. I picked a fight with him and let him draw his gun first. Then I killed him."

Ginny was silent. Many compulsions, she knew, drove men to the things they did. She wished she had known this about Curt before. She said: "I'm sorry, Curt."

"Sorry? Don't be, because I'm not. I got my revenge against K Diamond, don't you understand?" He stared down at her impatiently.

Ginny understood well enough. Curt had got his revenge, all right, but it had hurt him more than it helped. She said: "Why did you leave?"

His voice was bitter. "The coroner cleared me. Self-defense. But the people didn't. They treated me like a lousy outcast. I was a killer. Even the ones I'd helped didn't want anything to do with me. So I pulled out. The devil with them!"

"And why did you come back?"

He touched her for the first time. He gripped her small shoulders so hard that she had to bite her lip to keep from crying out. "Why did I come back? I'll tell you why. Because this stinking country owes me something. Because I want it now. I'm tired of going from one lousy town to another, from one lousy gun job to another. I can see the end, Ginny, and it isn't very pretty."

She felt a stir of compassion. "All right, Curt. But you can't tear what you think they owe you from them by force. You have to earn it. From what I've heard, K Diamond isn't a bad outfit now. They haven't bothered anybody in more than three years."

He chuckled savagely. "I've bothered them, though."

Ginny felt a cold chill along her spine. She asked, in a still, even voice: "Curt, did you put Tony Lazzeri up to fencing that valley?"

"What if I did?" His tone was openly defiant.

"Then you're the one who killed him."

Curt threw her violently away from him. She tripped and almost fell. He was trembling visibly with his rage. "Don't say that!"

"Curt, can't you see? Maybe you didn't pull the trigger. But you're to blame because he's dead. Stop, Curt, please! While you still can."

She could not quite understand his relief. He said easily:

"Ginny, this is man's business. Go on back to the hotel and stay out of it."

She shrugged resignedly, now thoroughly confused and bewildered. "All right, Curt."

He took her arm and together they retraced their steps along the darkened and almost deserted main street. At the hotel, Ginny pulled away and went up the steps. And Curt returned purposefully toward the saloon.

Ginny went into the hotel dining room, although she was not particularly hungry. She sat down at a wall table and stared moodily before her. She felt thoroughly disillusioned. For Curt had let her believe he was coming to Whitewater for a new start, an honest job, and a chance to discard the gun as a way of life. He had let her believe he would send for her or come after her. Now she realized that he'd had no such intention. The wordless way he'd left her at the hotel steps told her that, if nothing else did. She was part of his past, part of what he wanted to forget.

VIII

Curt was still irritated as he shouldered into the Mesa Saloon. Facing the cause of his irritation, he wondered if he had ever intended either sending for Ginny or returning for her. With a wry smile, he decided that it had more or less depended upon what happened here in Whitewater after he arrived.

It had depended as well upon Ellen Santangelo, on whether or not she was yet married, on what her reaction to his return was, perhaps, too, on what success he achieved with his plans here. Now, suddenly, he decided that he did not want Ginny. She was part of his past, the past he wanted to forget. She was a girl who had worked in saloons and whose reputation was naturally tarnished from the association.

Curt was convinced that Ginny was a good girl, a moral girl who had been forced into saloon work to survive. Yet he also was convinced that she would never quite live down the stigma of her former employment.

His own mind actually was as confused as Ginny's. With scowling concentration, he poured himself a drink and stared at it while he tried to unscramble his confused desires. Around him the senseless, half-drunken babble of the small cowmen went on unnoticed, a jubilant battle, for all of them sensed that K Diamond was dying, that it was going to be sliced like a pie and that each would get a piece.

Primarily, Curt decided, his return had been an effort to escape the squalor, degradation, and inevitable consequences of his way of life. He had thought of Ellen more as a means to that end than as a woman. He had really believed he could accomplish his purpose here in Whitewater without more killing, and he regretted the fact that he had let Rennick talk him into killing Tony. And he felt vaguely angered, as though he realized he had let himself become Rennick's tool.

His mind said: *That's over, though. I'm my own man from here on out.*

Which brought to him the realization that no further plans had been made and that time was short. There was always the possibility, remote though it was, that the coroner would not name Kellman in the death of Tony Lazzeri.

Curt's eyes roved along the bar and settled on Rennick. Rennick was not drunk, but there was the unaccustomed flush of alcohol and success upon his unshaven face. His eyes glittered oddly.

Curt caught his attention and beckoned. He stepped away from the bar and, as Rennick approached, said: "Kellman may not stay in jail. You can never tell about Wade Daugherty. I think we'd better make some plans so that we can get busy in the morning."

Rennick seemed to make an effort to shake off the numbing

effects of the alcohol he had consumed. He nodded owlishly. "You're right."

Curt said: "Go back to the card room and light the lamp. I'll bring Sontag and Pierce and Carter. That's enough for a start."

Rennick moved away and Curt went along the bar, touching the arm of each man he had named and beckoning with a toss of his head. With three of them following, he headed back between the pool tables to the open door of the card room. Rennick was lighting a lamp inside. Curt stood aside, let Sontag, Pierce, and Carter enter, then closed the door behind him.

He said abruptly: "We've got them on the run. Kellman's in jail, and now's the time to get moving."

Sontag rumbled: "What you figure to do first?"

Curt looked from one to the other, gauging their drunkenness and deciding it was not great enough to affect their thoughts seriously. He said: "The four of you live above K Diamond. Tomorrow I want all of you to meet at Rennick's. Bring your help if you've got any, and anyone else you can trust. But I don't want this to get out."

Sontag rumbled: "What are we going to do?"

"We're going to gather everything above K Diamond . . . all the K Diamond stock that's above the home place. We'll drive them ahead of us. About a mile above K Diamond there's a narrow place in the valley. We'll run a fence across there, from rim to rim."

Pierce made a long, low whistle.

Curt said at once: "Isn't that better than each man trying to make his own grab independently of the rest? We can hold that fence. But we can't hold half a dozen scattered from one end of Cañon Creek to the other. Besides, Sam Kellman probably won't do a damned thing until after he's talked to Jess. And he won't know anything about what we're doing until he sees that herd of K Diamond stock coming down the valley."

Rennick seemed to have shaken off the effects of his drinking. He said: "Curt's right. We can hold a fence across Cañon Creek. And we'll have grabbed two-thirds of K Diamond in a single day." His eyes were glowing.

Pierce asked doubtfully: "Suppose Jesse Kellman gets out of jail?"

"He won't. But even if he does, what do you think he can do? Curt's got him buffaloed. And with five or six to back Curt, Kellman won't dare try anything."

"What about Wade Daugherty?" growled Sontag.

Curt's face flushed slightly. "To hell with Wade! What can he do? Nothing above the fence is deeded land. It's Public Domain. Wade can't interfere. But all of you remember this . . . we start no trouble. If there are going to be shots fired, let Kellman's bunch fire first. That way we'll be in the clear."

Rennick was grinning and licking his lips. He said: "Curt's right. The whole country's against Kellman now. Let's keep it that way."

Sontag said: "So we grab most of K Diamond. Who gets what when we do?"

Rennick looked at Curt, but Curt avoided his glance. He was scowling at Sontag. "Suppose we get the pie before we start cutting it up, huh?" And he held Sontag's glance with his own harsh stare until Sontag looked away. For he knew that bickering over the spoils now was the one single thing that could spoil the plan faster than anything else. Besides, the division of the spoils was already arranged between Rennick and himself. Sontag, Pierce, and Carter were only tools. If they got any part of K Diamond at all, it would be a damned small part. Rennick and Curt himself intended to have the bulk of it.

He moved toward the door and paused with his hand on the knob. "Daylight, then, at Rennick's. And have the good sense to keep your mouths shut about it, will you?"

Smiling, he watched them file past him into the saloon.

Wade Daugherty was vaguely uneasy as he mounted the steps to the Santangelos' porch. He kept telling himself that relations between himself and Ellen had been restored to normal by her visit this afternoon and by her apology. But he was not convinced. He could not help remembering the expression her face had held as she talked to Curt McVey in front of Prior's store afterward. And he could not help the angry, corrosive jealousy that slumbered in his brain.

But being a sensible man, and one not entirely unfamiliar with the vagaries of the female sex, he was aware that this was a crucial time in both his own and Ellen's life. He must be very careful to say nothing, to do nothing that would antagonize her and drive her to Curt. And yet there was that in him, vague and unformed, which wondered why a man needed to worry about driving his promised bride to another man.

He shook his head savagely. Doubt had no place in a man when he thought of the woman he intended to marry.

He twisted the bell with unnecessary vigor. Ellen herself opened the door, smiling rather uncertainly. Wade took off his hat and stepped into the parlor. Ellen would have turned away, but he caught her around the waist with one arm and pulled her to him.

Her kiss was perfunctory and cool. Wade felt a stir of anger, but forced it down and kept his smile steady. The air was rich with the smell of frying steak and baking pie. He sniffed appreciatively.

Ellen went back toward the kitchen, hurrying, and then Wade noticed Mike Santangelo sitting on the leather-covered parlor sofa.

"Hello, Mike."

Mike grinned at him amiably. He said: "Kellman give you

any trouble?"

"Uhn-uh."

"Open and shut, ain't it? He's guilty as hell."

Wade said: "I'm not so sure. There's a couple of things that don't add up."

Mike looked surprised, doubtful. "Like what?"

Wade sat down beside him. His eyes were worried. "Well, for one thing, the Kellmans' tracks going in showed they were hurrying. Coming out they took their time. For another, they left Rennick to testify against them."

Mike pulled at his lower lip. He murmured: "Wade, Kellman's no fool. He knows you're no fool, either. Maybe he did things like that for the reason that he wanted you to doubt."

Wade shrugged wearily. "Maybe."

"Besides, if Kellman didn't do it, who did?"

Wade looked warily toward the kitchen. "Curt. Rennick is a hot-tempered little fool, but he hasn't got the guts to shoot a man down in cold blood. Curt packs a Forty-Four just like Kellman does. And it's mighty blamed convenient just now for Curt and Rennick to have Jesse Kellman locked up in jail. I figure they're going to make a grab for K Diamond. They know Sam Kellman is too dumb to give them very much trouble. But Jesse's different."

"What're you going to do?"

"I don't know, Mike. I'm blamed if I know. It doesn't seem fair to Kellman to keep him locked up while Curt and Rennick take K Diamond away from him. He'll never get it back if they do, you know."

Mike's face was thoughtful, serious. He said: "Wade, let it alone. You've done your duty, which was to bring in Kellman after Rennick made his accusation. Don't torment yourself wondering if you're right or not. Because you are right. You've done all anyone could expect you to do."

"But what if Kellman isn't guilty?"

"He's guilty, all right. But even if he ain't, it's for a jury to decide, ain't it?"

Mike's philosophy was convenient. And for a moment, Wade caught himself wanting to accept it. It would be so much easier if he did. Easier, and safer all around.

From the dining room Ellen called—"Come on, you two!"— and Wade got to his feet.

Wade was a tall man who was not at all handsome. Yet there was that about him a certain ruggedness and virility, which was a sort of handsomeness in itself. His face was somber as he took his seat at the table, his deep-set eyes troubled.

Ellen took a chair across from him and smiled at him uncertainly. "You look awfully glum tonight."

He nodded, looking at her thoughtfully. "I am."

"What's the matter?"

"Tony, I guess. He wasn't the kind to get into the sort of trouble he did. The whole thing's got a bad smell, and I guess I won't feel right about it until I get it straightened out."

There was coolness suddenly in Ellen's smooth face. She said evenly: "Why don't you let it alone? You've got Kellman, and Gil Rennick says he saw Kellman shoot Tony. What more do you want?"

Wade felt an odd stubbornness coming over him. It was becoming plain that no one agreed with him. Everyone thought Kellman guilty, and was either secretly or openly pleased to see him in jail.

Curt had become more already than a gunman returning home. He had become a champion of the poor, a kind of Robin Hood. Wade knew uneasily that he should change the subject, but his new stubbornness prevented it. He said: "What if Kellman's innocent?"

Ellen looked at him levelly. "What are you trying to say, Wade?

If Kellman's innocent, then who is guilty?"

Mike interrupted: "Ellen, you forgot to put the salt on the table. Darn it. . . ."

Ellen picked up the saltshaker and handed it to him. "Here it is, Dad."

Mike took it irritably. He said: "Why don't you two find something else to talk about? I'm sick of hearing about Tony and Kellman and Rennick. Besides, it's not exactly the sort of thing you discuss at the dinner table."

Ellen smiled at him in a thin way. She said with mock dutifulness: "Yes, Father."

For a while the three ate in silence, but there was little enjoyment in any of them even though the food was excellent. Wade and Mike finished, and Ellen rose and went into the kitchen for the pie. Mike got up and began to pick up the dishes from the table.

After a few moments, Ellen returned. Wade looked up at her, and for a moment his eyes met her glance steadily. He felt a sinking sensation as he saw the hostility in her eyes.

She sat down across from him and the three finished the pie in silence and without comment.

At last Wade said: "Ellen, I'm not going to beat around the bush any more. Curt's coming back seems to have caused trouble between us and we'd just as well face it."

"All right, Wade. Suppose we do face it."

Mike broke in savagely: "Stop it, you two!"

Wade glanced at him shortly, then back to Ellen. He said: "I'll tell you what I think. I don't think Kellman is guilty. I think Rennick and Curt set this up, talked Tony into grabbing Deer Creek in a deliberate attempt to draw Kellman into moving against him. Maybe they figured Kellman would kill Tony. When he didn't, either Curt or Rennick killed him instead."

For a long moment Ellen stared at him in silence, dislike

coming into her face, a fact that mildly amazed him. At last she said: "Now I'll tell you what I think. I think you're jealous of Curt. I think being sheriff has gone to your head, although I can't imagine why. There isn't a dirtier, more underpaid job in the county. I think I'm glad this has come out when it did. Because I'm not at all sure that I want to marry you. What's in it for me, anyway? A lifetime of scraping along on a sheriff's pay? I'll tell you something else, Wade. If you release Kellman, we're through. Because I won't stand for your persecuting Curt. Do I make myself clear?"

Wade rose. He wanted suddenly to get out of there, quickly. He said softly: "You make yourself very clear. Thanks for the supper, Ellen. Good night."

He turned and headed for the front door. He took down his hat and coat from the coat tree without looking back.

He could almost feel the shocked silence behind him. Mike got out uncertainly: "I wish you two would calm down."

But Ellen said nothing, and Wade did not look back. He opened the door, stepped out onto the porch, and closed the door behind him.

Going down the walk, he was suddenly, wildly angry.

IX

On the way to the jail, Wade stopped at a small frame house set back from the street almost to the alley. He walked through the high weeds along the path and knocked heavily on the door.

It opened, and a small, wiry man in shirt sleeves and vest stood framed in it. Wade said: "Hello, John. You want to work tonight?"

John Ryorsen stepped away from the door, saying: "Come in, Wade. I figured you'd want me tonight. Heard you had Kellman locked up and I knew you'd want someone to stay there with him."

Wade went in and waited while John Ryorsen shrugged into his threadbare black coat.

Ryorsen had been sheriff of Whitewater County and Wade had been his deputy. When Ryorsen had decided he wanted to retire, Wade had run in his place and had been elected. Now Wade used John Ryorsen as night jailer and deputy whenever he needed an extra man.

Ryorsen belted on his gun, crammed a shapeless hat onto his graying, balding head. He leaned over the lamp and blew it out. He said: "Let's go."

Wade stepped out into the darkness.

Ryorsen came after him and closed the door. He said: "So you got Jesse Kellman. I always figured Jesse had more sense than to step into something like this, but maybe I was wrong."

"You weren't wrong. I think somebody's making a fool out of both Jesse and me. He didn't kill Tony."

"You sound pretty sure." Ryorsen's voice held a note of surprise.

"I'm as sure as ever a man is." He told John Ryorsen about the tracks he had seen, the tracks of the Kellmans both going in and coming out of the Deer Creek Valley. He told about Kellman's convincing show of innocence. He said: "I ought to turn him loose."

"But you can't. You know that. You've got a complaining witness that says he saw Kellman kill Tony. You've got no choice, Wade."

"Unless I make a choice."

"Don't stick your neck out, Wade. There's hardly a man in Whitewater County that isn't convinced that Kellman's guilty. You turn him loose and you'll lose a lot of votes."

Wade's mouth made a bitter twist. "And if I don't, Kellman will lose K Diamond. You see any justice in that?"

Ryorsen said patiently: "You're the sheriff, Wade. You've done what you're supposed to do. The rest is up to the courts. Call in Doc Sayers tomorrow for a coroner's inquest if you want. Maybe that'll make you feel better about it."

"And Doc will name Kellman. How will that help things?"

They were walking along the street now, heading for the lights of the hotel. Ryorsen said: "It'll take the load off your shoulders. Ain't that what you want?"

Wade stopped. "No, hang it. That isn't what I want at all. I don't care about crawling out from under. I want to do what's right. If Kellman didn't kill Tony, I don't want him in my jail. If Curt or Rennick did, then I want them instead of Kellman."

Ryorsen was silent for a moment. At last he said: "Then by hell get going and find out who did kill Tony."

Wade smiled sourly. "You make it sound so easy."

They reached the sheriff's office and Wade unlocked the door. He went through the office and opened the door into the jail. On the shelf, the lamp was smoking. Wade trimmed the wick. Kellman was stretched out on the bunk. He watched Wade steadily with his narrowed eyes. Wade asked: "Everything all right, Jess?"

Kellman didn't answer. Wade went into the cell and got the empty supper dishes. He carried them out and relocked the door. He said: "John Ryorsen will be staying here tonight. If you want anything, just holler."

"There's only one thing I want. That's out of here."

Wade didn't reply. He carried the tray of dishes out the door and into the street. Thoughtful and depressed, he crossed to the hotel. He carried the dishes into the kitchen and set them down. When he got back to the lobby, the clerk beckoned to him.

"That new girl, Miss Ginny Martin, left word that she wanted to see you."

Wade fished his watch from his pocket and looked at the time. 8:00 p.m. He crossed to the stairs, and, as he did, the clerk called after him: "Two-Oh-Four is the room number!"

Wade went upstairs and searched along the dark hall until he came to room 204. He knocked on the door and immediately heard a stir of movement inside the room.

The door opened and the girl, Ginny Martin, stood in it smiling faintly and uncertainly.

Wade said: "You wanted to see me?"

"Yes. Won't you come in?"

Wade went in, carefully leaving the door ajar behind him, an action Ginny did not fail to notice.

She gestured toward the room's single chair, and then sat nervously on the edge of the bed. Wade sat down and laid his hat on the floor.

She murmured: "I don't quite know how to start."

Wade waited.

At last she said uncertainly: "Curt and I were to have been married. He was going to come back here, put away his guns, and make a new start. He said he thought he could get a job with one of the smaller cowmen here, one of those he had helped by what he did three years ago."

Wade didn't know exactly what to say. So he said nothing. He felt a vast sympathy for this girl.

She said, her eyes very soft: "I wanted to get away from what I was doing and I thought Curt did, too. Maybe that was the trouble. I guess all we both wanted was a new kind of life. Maybe we didn't love each other at all."

Wade said without really believing it: "Curt may have tried. Maybe he tried to get a job from Rennick. Probably it isn't Curt's fault that it didn't work out the way he wanted it to. You've got to remember that every small cowman in Whitewater County hates K Diamond. And Rennick saw in Curt a chance to get even."

She smiled at him wearily. "You don't really believe that."

Her eyes were honest, candid, and he shook his head. He said: "No. I guess I know Curt too well. He's sick of living by his guns, but he isn't above using them to get something out of this country that he figures is coming to him."

Ginny flushed a little as she said: "He's trying to take Ellen Santangelo from you, isn't he?"

Wade said wryly: "He's doing a good job of it, too." Suddenly defensive, he asked: "What was it you wanted to see me about?"

"Can't you drive him out of town? Can't you say that he's an undesirable and just force him to leave?"

Wade nodded. "I could. But that wouldn't help either you or me. I'd get Ellen, and you'd probably get Curt. But would either of us ever be quite satisfied? Wouldn't we always wonder?"

Ginny smiled reluctantly. She murmured: "You've got more courage than I have, I guess."

"I doubt that." Wade was feeling a strong attraction toward this girl, an attraction that made him momentarily forget Ellen. He stood up. She stood, too, and for a moment they faced each other. Wade said regretfully: "You're going to hate me before this is over, because I've got a feeling I'm going to kill Curt. If he doesn't kill me first."

She watched his face, as though trying to memorize it. Her eyes were wide and defenseless. Wade turned abruptly and went out of the room.

Going down the stairs, he was thoughtful and depressed, for he knew there was nothing ahead for Ginny Martin save heartbreak if she clung to Curt, heartbreak if she lost him.

He came into the lobby, and several men in business suits rose from the leather-covered settee and approached him. One of them was Wilbur Prior.

Prior besides being a storekeeper was mayor of the town, and Wade suddenly realized that the men with him were the members of the town council. Wade made a dry smile.

Prior coughed hesitantly. "Wade, we'd like to talk to you."

"All right."

"It's about Jesse Kellman. We'd hate to see you turn him loose, and we've heard talk that you're thinking of doing just that."

"Been talking to John Ryorsen? Or to Mike Santangelo?"

"Mike. He was in the store a few minutes ago."

"You must have moved fast, then, to get the council together this quickly."

Prior gave him a disapproving stare. "We want to know what your stand is, Wade. If you turn Kellman loose, there'll be hell to pay all over the county." Prior's face was getting progressively pinker.

Wade asked: "Why will there be hell to pay, Wilbur?"

"You know that as well as we do."

"Suppose you tell me." He was deliberately taunting Prior to anger now, wondering what the man knew and hoping he'd spill it.

Prior rose to the bait. "Why, Wade, you know Tony's fencing of Deer Creek Valley was only a beginning. Tomorrow. . . ."

"Tomorrow what?"

"Nothing." Prior's mouth snapped shut like a trap.

Wade grinned. "That's what I thought. Tomorrow they make their big grab for K Diamond, is that it? And you're afraid if Kellman's loose, they won't make it stick? What's your stake in this, gentlemen? Business? Kellman ships in his supplies from the wholesale houses in Denver by rail. And you figure that if the small cowmen take over K Diamond, your business will increase. Is that it?"

There was anger in the faces of the men confronting him now. Anger because Wade had put his finger on the truth. They started to bluster, but Wade cut them short. "How'd you find out they were going to grab K Diamond tomorrow? Somebody blab?"

Prior blurted: "Well, Pierce was in for cartridges. . . ."

Another man said intemperately: "Sheriff, neither the mayor nor the town council of Whitewater has any authority over you. You're a county official. But think twice before you do anything rash, like turning Kellman loose. You'll bathe the country in blood if you do."

Wade stared at him, hard. He let his stare wander coldly over the face of each man in the group. Finally he said: "You're right. You have no authority over me, and I'm a county official. I'm supposed to be just. Is it just to leave a man lie in jail when I honestly believe him innocent while his neighbors steal everything he has?" Prior started to speak, but Wade stopped him. "You're going to say now that I'm an elected official. That I won't be sheriff next term if I turn the people against me. Well, let me tell you something. If I lose votes by doing what I believe to be right, then I won't be sheriff next term. And I won't care. Because I won't be told how to do my duty. Is that clear, gentlemen?"

One or two of them nodded reluctantly.

Wade said: "Excuse me, then. I've got things to do."

He turned on his heel and went out toward the street. He paused before the hotel, fishing absently for his pipe. He packed it carefully and touched a match to its bowl. Puffing thoughtfully, he walked downstreet toward the railroad station. He kept going over the facts of Tony Lazzeri's killing in his mind, sorting, discarding, trying to fit them together into some kind of pattern.

Rennick had been with Tony, according to Rennick's story. And Curt had gone to Tony's for fence stretchers.

Suddenly Wade stopped abruptly. Fence stretchers. That was

one item he hadn't seen at the place where he'd found Tony's body.

Wade turned and headed for the Mesa Saloon. He went inside. Curt McVey sat alone at a table. All of the small cowmen seemed to have gone home. There was, besides Curt, only a handful of townsmen in the saloon.

Curt was idly playing solitaire with a dog-eared pack of cards. There was no drink before him. Wade went over, pulled out a chair, and sat down. He said: "I'm trying to straighten out a few things in my mind. Mind if I ask you a few questions?"

Curt said guardedly: "No. Why should I?"

"Good. Now, first of all, did you hear the shot that killed Tony?"

Curt appeared to be considering. Finally he said: "I might have. Come to think of it, I guess I did. I heard something when I was about halfway between the fence and Tony's shack."

"Going toward it or coming back?"

"Coming back. I got the fence stretchers and. . . ."

Wade interrupted: "What'd you do with them, by the way?"

For the first time Curt was flustered. He said: "Hell, I don't remember. Dropped 'em, I guess."

"And when you got to Tony's body, the Kellmans were gone?" Wade tried hard to conceal his satisfaction by asking this innocent question.

He listened to Curt's answer with only part of his mind. He was convinced that there had been no fence stretchers. And if there was one lie in Rennick's story, then it was probably a fabrication of lies. At least, if he could prove this part of it a lie, he would have justification for releasing Kellman, if not for arresting Curt.

He talked idly with Curt for a few moments about things unconnected with the killing to allay Curt's suspicions, and then excused himself.

Outside the saloon again, he headed directly for the livery barn. He got his horse from the drowsy hostler, Russ Fagin, and rode out of town.

Tony Lazzeri had had few close friends. But if anyone would know about the fence stretchers, it would be Tony's nearest neighbor, Hughie Peterson. It was toward Hughie's place that Wade rode.

He pushed the horse steadily for the better part of an hour, and finally rode into Peterson's yard.

The house, a tiny, poorly built log affair, was dark. Wade dismounted and hammered on the door.

He heard a woman's querulous voice, and a shuffling of feet. Then a lamp glowed, and the door opened. Hughie Peterson, wiry and stooped, stood framed in it, clad in a long, red-flannel nightshirt.

"Sheriff! It's you, huh? What the devil you want this time of night?"

"A little information, if you don't mind, Hughie. About Tony. You used to borrow tools and machinery from him, didn't you?"

"Sure. Everybody knows that. He borrowed stuff from me, too."

"You'd know about everything he had around his place, then, wouldn't you?"

"I been there often enough. I ought to."

"He have any fence stretchers?"

"Hell no! Tony used a hammer to stretch wire. Just like I do. I've seen him use a hammer a hundred times. What would he want with wire stretchers?"

Wade grinned. "Thanks, Hughie. Go on back to bed. That's all I wanted to know."

Peterson looked at him as though he thought Wade were crazy. He said in an indignant tone: "You rode all the way up here from town an' got me out of bed just to ask me that?

Sheriff, you crazy or something?"

Wade's grin widened. "No, I'm not crazy, Hughie. Go on back to bed. Sorry I bothered you."

Peterson grumbled for a moment, then slammed the door viciously. Wade got his horse, mounted, and set out for town.

He'd got what he needed, and he ought to have been feeling satisfied. But somehow he didn't. All he could think of now was tomorrow, of the blood that would spill when Curt's and Kellman's forces came together. And of how he had to stop it somehow, all by himself.

X

It was a little after 10:00 p.m. when Wade got back to town. He put his horse up at the livery stable, unsaddling and rubbing down the animal briskly with an old gunny sack.

Most of the town was dark at this hour. There were a few scattered lights in the hotel, in the Mesa Saloon, and in the sheriff's office.

Wade walked briskly along Main and turned off a block above the hotel. Half a block along this street, he came to the tiny frame shack where Doc Sayers lived his bachelor's existence. The windows were dark.

Wade pounded on the door, hoping that Doc wasn't so drunk that he couldn't be wakened. Apparently he was not, for a few moments of pounding brought Doc's sleepy, protesting, querulous voice.

The door opened and Wade could see the blur of Doc's white nightshirt. He said: "I want to talk to you."

"Now? Hang it, Sheriff, can't it wait till morning?"

"Afraid not. Light a lamp, Doc."

Doc moved away from the door and struck a match. He held it to the lamp wick, and then lowered the chimney.

Wade went in. He said: "I want you to do me a favor."

Doc scratched his unshaven jaw.

Wade said: "I want you to hold an inquest first thing in the morning. I want you to call it death at the hands of person or persons unknown."

Doc said plaintively: "Hell, I can't do that. You've got a suspect in jail."

"I won't have by morning. I'm going to turn him loose."

For a moment, Doc stared at him. The drowsiness went out of his eyes, to be replaced by a sharp, shrewd look that Wade seldom saw there these days.

Doc said: "You sure you know what you're doing? Curt and Rennick and some of the others had their heads together in the saloon tonight. I'd say they're planning a grab for tomorrow. If Kellman's loose when they do, there's going to be hell to pay."

"I figure on stopping that."

Doc peered at him worriedly. "You're a fool. You take your job too seriously. Why should you step between them?"

"The law is supposed to keep the peace, isn't it?"

"Sure, but you can't stop a bunch like that one."

Wade said wearily: "I've made up my mind. I don't want to argue, Doc. Will you do it?"

Doc crossed the room, fumbled under the mattress for a moment, and came back with a half-empty bottle. He asked: "Drink?"

Wade shook his head.

Doc asked: "Mind if I do?"

Again Wade shook his head.

Doc tipped up the bottle and took a long drink. He said: "On the evidence, I ought to name Kellman. You know anything else that I don't?"

Wade said doubtfully: "You'll keep it strictly to yourself?"

Doc nodded.

Wade said: "Curt was supposed to have been at Tony's getting wire stretchers when Tony was killed. I found out tonight that Tony never had any wire stretchers."

Doc said uncertainly: "That's a blamed small point to stand on."

"It proves something, though. Something I've suspected all along. It proves that Curt and Rennick were lying. It proves to me at least that Curt was there all the time. Before I'm through, maybe it'll prove that Curt did the killing instead of Kellman."

"Still trying to hang something on Curt, aren't you? You know what the town and what Ellen will say to that accusation, don't you?"

Wade grinned sourly. "Sure. They'll say I'm persecuting Curt for personal reasons."

"Are you?"

Wade's grin faded. "If I were, I'd do it a lot easier than I'm doing. I'd just run him out of town." He was getting nervous, impatient. He said: "Doc, I'm turning Kellman loose tonight. Whether you go along with me on this or not. It'll just make it easier all around if you do go along. What do you say?"

Doc nodded reluctantly. "All right. I'll do it. I'll say you've got evidence that proves Kellman didn't do it. It'll be up to you to dig up that evidence before you get back to town tomorrow."

Wade shrugged. He said meagerly: "Thanks, Doc." And went out into the night.

He was irritated and confused. Everybody seemed intent on making it hard for him. Everybody was taking Curt McVey's side, and Curt didn't deserve their consideration. Wade was convinced now that Curt had shot Tony Lazzeri in cold blood. But he still had to prove it. And he faced a much more serious task, that of preventing open war tomorrow over K Diamond's vast range.

He went over to the sheriff's office and went inside. John Ryorsen was dozing in the swivel chair, his feet on the desk. He sat up as Wade came in.

Wade said: "I'm turning Kellman loose. You can go home, John." Ryorsen started to speak, but Wade stopped him with an impatient wave of his hand. "Never mind. My mind's made up, and I won't change it. Besides, I'm getting awful tired of being told how to run the sheriff's office."

Ryorsen said: "Easy, now. Easy. Don't get on the prod about it."

Wade grinned. "Sorry. But, by Judas, every man in this town has put his two cents' worth into this business today. I'm getting tired of it, I guess."

He opened the door and went back into the cell-block. Kellman stared at him impassively. Wade unlocked the door, went in, and sat down on the bench beside Kellman. He said: "Jess, they're figuring to grab K Diamond tomorrow. I'll let you go, but I want you to play along with me."

Something flared in Kellman's deep-set eyes, then died. He eyed Wade suspiciously. "What do you mean, play along with you? They're not going to get K Diamond. If you think I'll stand by and let them, then you'd just as well keep me here."

Wade said: "Let me ride with you. And don't open fire until they do. Will you go that far?"

He watched Kellman closely, not missing the stubborn set of the big man's jaw, the unyielding look in his eyes. At last Kellman shrugged. "All right. I'll go that far. I guess you're trying to do the right thing, Wade. Ryorsen told me how much pressure they're putting on you."

Wade murmured: "Jess, take a tip from me. If we get this straightened out, stop buying your supplies over in Denver. Buy them locally. Then maybe they won't all be against you." He stood up and gestured toward the open door.

Kellman went out. He halted uncertainly in the office, looking first at Wade, and then at Ryorsen. Wade got Kellman's gun from the nail where he'd hung it and handed it to the big man. "I'll walk down to the stable with you while you get your horse. And I'll be at your place at dawn. Wait for me."

Kellman grunted: "Sure." He stuffed his gun into his belt. He hesitated a moment more and finally said: "Wade, thanks. I. . . ."

"Forget it. Come on, let's go."

He followed Kellman out into the night, leaving Ryorsen behind, shaking his head doubtfully.

The liveryman was asleep in his tack room bunk, a fact for which Wade was duly grateful. He helped Kellman get his horse, and then watched him ride out of town. So far as he could tell, no one saw Kellman leave.

Wondering if he had been right, Wade went to the hotel, through the deserted lobby, and up the stairs to his room.

He removed only his boots and lay down on the bed fully clothed. But he did not sleep, for his mind was too busy. Busy with doubts as to the wisdom of what he had done, doubts that any one man could stop the carnage that was planned for tomorrow.

Later, when his mind tired of the repetition of these thoughts, he found himself remembering the girl, Ginny Martin, and unconsciously comparing her with Ellen. . . .

At last he slept.

Wade was up two hours before daylight. He washed his face and combed his hair, then slipped on his boots and coat. Carrying his hat, he went quickly out into the hall.

Down at the other end of it another door opened and Ginny Martin came out, fully dressed in a split riding skirt and short sheepskin jacket. Wade frowned, but he waited for her, and they went down the stairs into the darkened lobby together.

Outside in the chill street, Wade said with puzzlement: "You're up early."

She nodded, unsmiling.

Wade said: "Would it be prying to ask you where you're going?"

"Not at all. I'm going for a ride. Up Cañon Creek."

"Oh, no, you're not."

Now her lips curved into a faintly mocking smile. "How do you propose to stop me?"

For a moment he stared at her with plain unfriendliness. Then reluctantly he grinned. "You're a blackmailer. Seriously, though, I can't let you go up there today. There's going to be trouble."

"I know. That's why I'm going."

"You hope to stop it? By appealing to Curt?"

She shook her head. "I know better than that. But perhaps men will be hurt. I can help them."

Wade felt a stir of admiration. And had a new thought: *Why not?* He shrugged. "All right. On one condition. You do exactly as I say without question."

Ginny nodded agreement. Together, then, they walked along the still, dark street until they came to the livery barn. And ten minutes later rode back through town and out on the Cañon Creek road.

Wade wondered why his thoughts were clearer in this girl's presence. She said nothing, and she rarely glanced at him as they rode, yet there was a deep sense of companionship in Wade, a sense of contentment he had never experienced with Ellen.

Looking back now on the past three years, he realized that Ellen had been putting him off not because she was unready for marriage, but because she cherished in her heart a secret longing for Curt, and a hope that he would return. Her readiness to quarrel with Wade, to defend Curt, and to turn to him amply demonstrated that. Yet Wade, realizing that he had never really had Ellen, did not feel the sense of loss that he might otherwise have.

As they rode, the eastern sky above the high rims turned a cold gray. Light touched the brush of the valley. The sky was turning pink as they rode into the Kellmans' yard.

The place this morning had the appearance of a ranch at roundup time. Every hand was out, saddled and ready, and each carried, in addition to his holstered revolver, a rifle, either cradled in his arms or shoved down into a saddle boot.

Kellman was waiting impatiently, sitting astride a big gray gelding. His brother Sam, also mounted, waited dumbly beside him, trying only to stay out of his way.

Kellman rode over and confronted Wade. "It's about time you got here!" He looked at Ginny and his scowl deepened. "What the devil is she doing here?"

Ginny met his unfriendly stare calmly. She said: "Have you got the wagon hitched up?"

"What wagon?"

"Why, the wagon to bring back the wounded, of course. What else?"

Dumbfounded, Kellman did not answer.

Ginny said sweetly: "You don't mean to tell me you didn't think of that? Or don't you think there will be any fighting?"

"There'll be fighting, all right."

"Then get a wagon or buckboard ready. Put some blankets in the bed of it, and some clean sheets for bandages."

Kellman's face darkened. "Hanged if I will!"

Ginny said softly: "Look around at your men."

Kellman did. He cursed. But he ordered Sam to get the buckboard hitched up and to provide blankets and sheets as Ginny had instructed. He delegated an oldster to drive the rig and ordered Ginny to stay with it.

Then he turned to Wade. "Is there any special way you want

to handle this?"

Wade shrugged. He didn't have the slightest idea how Curt and Rennick planned their steal. But it seemed reasonable that they'd first push the K Diamond cattle off the land they intended to take. That meant a drive down Cañon Creek to some point where they would cross the valley with a fence.

He outlined his idea briefly to Kellman, who nodded. "It'll take them a while to gather all the side cañons. But if we can surprise them before they get set. . . ."

Wade said: "Maybe we can. Let's go."

He threw a glance toward Ginny, who was waiting for Sam to bring the buckboard. He caught her watching him, a wholly unreadable expression in her eyes.

He followed Kellman out of the yard and the crew lined out behind. Wade felt oddly disturbed by the memory of Ginny, and of the way she had been watching him. It turned his thoughts personal, and he knew a strange, growing excitement that he tried resolutely to stifle. Ginny was Curt's woman. Or was she? No more than Ellen was his, Wade decided.

They went out the lane, holding their mounts at a walk. The crew called back and forth to one another, but their jests were forced and brittle. They were cowmen, not gunfighters, and Wade knew each of them was wondering whether he would be riding back tonight astride his horse, or whether he would be riding back in the buckboard.

With agonizing slowness the miles dropped behind. The buckboard caught up and now followed half a mile back, neither losing ground nor catching up.

Yet neither Wade nor Kellman were disposed to hurry. Later, they might need all the freshness and strength their horses possessed, and they would not waste it now in futile hurrying.

They approached the side cañon that contained Rennick's spread and Wade left the road, cut over, and scouted the mouth of the cañon. He picked up the tracks of a pair of loping horses headed upcountry and knew at last that he had not been mistaken in his guess as to Rennick's and Curt's plans. For these were their horses and the tracks had been made no more than two hours before.

As the morning progressed, the air turned warmer, and there was a new smell to it, that smell of earthiness peculiar to spring. A warm breeze stirred, blowing up from the south.

Perhaps this breeze delayed their hearing the cattle ahead. As it was, they were no more than a quarter mile away, hidden temporarily by a thicket of oak brush, when they caught the first low rumble of their bawling.

Wade halted instantly and signed for those behind him to do likewise. He turned to Kellman. "Stay here under cover. I'll ride out and talk to them."

Kellman blustered: "Damn it, that's my herd they're moving. I'll. . . ."

Wade's voice was like ice. "You'll do exactly as I tell you." He stared at Kellman with unblinking eyes. Kellman subsided, grumbling.

Wade rode out of the thicket into the open. Ahead of him was a long, slow rise, and, beyond that, he judged, the cattle were bunched. He kicked his horse's sides and rode at a fast trot to the crest of the rise.

XI

Below him now, he saw the cattle, several hundred of them, spread out almost the width of the valley. The drovers were having trouble with them due to the fact that many of the cows had small newborn calves that could not travel either fast or very far. Wade could hear Rennick's high, whining voice, Curt's shout, whistles, and the slapping of chaps with reins. He saw five men.

They saw him then, and instantly the valley was silent, save for the endless plaintive bawling of the cows that had lost their calves back in the drag of the herd.

Deliberately and slowly, Wade rode down toward them. He eased his horse through the bunched cattle, noting that Rennick's men had come together. He rode to within ten feet of them, and stopped. He said, looking at Curt: "The game's up. Jesse Kellman is back on the other side of that rise with Sam and six riders."

He saw the wildness, the viciousness rising in Curt. He saw the fright, the desperation in Rennick. The others were sheepish and uneasy.

Looking at Curt, he could almost see the man's thoughts at work. And he knew that Curt would not give up this easily.

So he pushed a little more. He said: "Curt, you've got twenty-four hours to get out of Whitewater County. If you're not gone in that time, I'll get Kellman to swear out a rustling complaint and I'll serve it."

Out of the corner of his eye, he saw a couple of white-faced bulls horning each other and pawing the ground. One was a big oldster that must have weighed 1,700 or 1,800 pounds. The other was a younger bull. They were coming closer with the larger bull crowding the smaller one mercilessly.

Wade felt a grim touch of uneasiness but he did not take his glance from Curt. Wade had handled cattle for years before he'd become sheriff. He knew that in a moment now that younger bull was going to break and run. And he also knew that when a bull ran, he was blind, unseeing, and that he would deviate not one inch from anything in his path. Wade had seen horses bowled over. He had even seen bulls run through fences and into trees.

The tension of the moment grew. Curt glanced at Rennick and some sort of signal seemed to pass between them.

Wade saw the tensing in Curt and let his hand touch the grips of his holstered revolver. He caught a blur of movement behind him and off to one side but he dared not take his glance from Curt. And then, with terrifying suddenness, something struck his horse's hindquarters.

It was the young bull, that had taken all the horning he could stand from the old one. His horn entered the fleshy part of Wade's horse's shoulder and flung him aside. The horse screamed and reared. Blood streamed from its shoulder. The animal lost its balance and fell over backward, with Wade trying desperately to free himself from the saddle in time.

Yet there was no time, and his attention had been on Curt, a fatal error. The horse crashed down, with Wade's leg pinned beneath the saddle.

Only the high pommel and cantle, and the saddle's solid construction, kept his leg from being smashed. As it was, he was pinned beneath the thrashing horse.

Wade could hear Rennick screaming: "Now! Curt, kill him now!"

Curt was laughing harshly. His voice was like a whip. "No! Not yet!"

One of the struggling horse's hoofs struck Wade in the side of the head. He could feel the warmth of blood immediately, and for an instant thereafter everything turned black. When he could see again, he was free, and Curt was kicking him viciously in the ribs.

"Get up! Get up, damn you! We'll see how good you fight today."

Wade struggled to his knees. Curt's knee smashed into his face and drove him back again. Rennick began to cackle with pure enjoyment. "That's it, Curt. Give it to him!"

Wade rolled, bunched his muscles, and surged to his feet. His eyes blurred, and his leg almost gave way beneath him. His ribs, where Curt had kicked him, pained excruciatingly. He turned, favoring the leg, in time to see Curt rushing at him, both hands swinging savagely.

Wade tried to duck, but he was too late and too slow on that hurt leg. One of Curt's blows landed flushly on his jaw, and again Wade went down. This time Curt landed atop him, punching with vicious concentration.

Wade knew the bitterness of total defeat. He could live so long as Curt was winning, was punishing him. But if he should, by any remote chance, begin to hold his own against Curt, then Rennick would shoot him. And the first shot would bring the Kellmans and their crew. He would be avenged, but that thought gave him little satisfaction. What he had tried so hard to avert, what he had promised to avert, would occur and the country would be bathed in blood.

It was not in Wade, however, to give up. Die he might, but he'd die fighting. He twisted away from Curt's torturing blows and, twisting more, brought up a knee into Curt's belly. He was rewarded by a grunt of pain.

Now the dizziness was beginning to go away and his mind was clearing. He fought free of Curt and came to his knees. Six feet away, Curt was doing likewise. But Wade, instead of rising, drove forward blindly, his head a battering ram that drove every bit of air from Curt's lungs in a sighing gust.

Rolling on the ground with Curt beneath him, Wade knew that for the first time he had the slightest of advantages. He grasped Curt's head by the hair and banged it savagely against the ground. But he was waiting all this time, waiting for the bite of Rennick's bullet.

He felt it smash into his shoulder and instantly afterward heard the deafening report, knowing from this that Rennick had fired from pointblank range.

The impact flung him aside, away from Curt. Out of a corner

of his eye, he saw Curt getting up. Curt gasped: "Wait! Damn you, Gil, I told you to wait. I ain't done with him yet!"

There was no particular pain in Wade's shoulder just now. Only a terrible numbness, only complete immobility. He could not raise his arm; he could not use it at all.

But shock dulled his mind, dulled his will to fight. Until Curt stepped forward and began again to kick him.

Rage began as an ember in the back of his brain. Like a grass fire in a high wind it mounted, until there was nothing important save that he smash Curt McVey.

His shoulder was soaked with blood. His leg was bruised and sprained until it would scarcely support his weight. His face was a bloody mass of bruises and he had two broken ribs. But he got up. He avoided Curt's boots and got up, and he stood, swaying, his face a study of uncontrolled fury. His eyes, so red and hating, found Rennick first, for in Rennick's fear lay the greatest danger.

He was on the man like a panther, bearing him back, wrenching the gun from him even as it exploded in his face. He did not even feel the sear of the bullet along his scalp. He wrenched the gun from Rennick and swiped at Rennick's head with it before he flung it away from him. He had no thought of guns now, for bullets could not give him quite the satisfaction he had to have.

Crouched, he glared around him, found Curt with his glance and rushed at the man. His savage attack completely unnerved Curt. Curt apparently believed that Wade had absorbed enough punishment to kill him, which indeed he had. Yet here he came, red-eyed and terrible, ignoring blood and crippling wounds.

Curt snatched for his gun. Hammer came back, and muzzle centered. And then Wade hit him.

The impact of their bodies was audible fifty feet away. Curt was flung back for all his weight, like a carelessly tossed ball. He fell into a stand of brush that held him partly upright. Wade came on, teeth bared a little, completely and wholly now a fighting animal.

This second charge broke Curt's spirit. Frantically he fought out of the entangling brush, frantically he ran to snatch the reins of the nearest horse, and instantly was mounted and galloping away.

There was no stopping Wade. With a bellow of frustrated rage he yanked Pierce from his saddle and leaped into it. His spurs sank into the startled animal's ribs. And he was thundering away, but a short fifty feet behind Curt.

Curt turned and emptied his gun at Wade. Then he crouched low on his horse's neck and reloaded with fumbling fingers, holding the reins in his teeth.

Up the valley they went, with Wade neither gaining ground nor losing it. A measure of sanity began to return to Wade with the rushing wind, but his rage did not lessen.

He knew it was important that he get back, that he stop the slaughter between the two opposing forces. But this was important, too. Curt had killed Tony in cold blood, and Curt must be made to pay.

They came at last, as they inevitably must, to a choking growth of brush, and here Curt had to slow. He shot a glance over his shoulder at Wade, and his eyes widened with what he saw. Wade was now but a scant thirty feet behind.

Instantly Curt flung himself from his horse. He hit the ground running, but halted quickly and whirled, his gun coming up to center.

Wade's gun was still in its holster. Like light, his hand flashed to it, his brain immediately realizing that in the gun now lay his only hope of life. There was not time to reach Curt. Only a bullet could reach him before he could fire.

Wade's was the disadvantage, for his horse was moving, coming to a halt with a hopping, jerking, sliding gait. Wade's gun came clear of leather, hammer back, leveled briefly, and fired.

Roaring its echo, Curt's gun fired. His bullet tugged at Wade's coat, scarcely noticed, for Wade's gun was firing now a second time. Both bullets struck Curt squarely and, coming so close together, drove him back as though he had been struck by a cannon ball. Still in his saddle, Wade watched him die. . . .

Rage so great is slow to die. And when it dies, it leaves a terrible, mountainous weariness. Added to this came the pain of Wade's wounds. But he could remember Kellman and the small ranchers, and the fighting building between them.

He became aware now of the sound of shots, and urged his horse to a gallop, returning downcountry to the scene of his fight with Curt.

He found Rennick and the others taking cover behind the low brush. Wade knew his own return, plus the news of Curt's death, might take the fight out of the settlers, so he yelled: "Rennick! Curt's dead!"

And the firing did stop, almost at once. Wade wondered if his strength would hold out long enough to see this through. He yelled: "Kellman, hold it!" And then called out to Rennick: "Gil, was it Curt that killed Tony?"

Silence greeted his question. He roared: "Damn you, was it?"

"Yeah. Yeah, it was Curt."

"Then get up and go on home. The whole damned pack of you. If you're not gone in two minutes, I'll let Kellman nail your hides to the barn door."

Sheepishly, frightened, they got up, hands in the air. They found their horses and mounted. Wade slid off Pierce's horse, and the man took the reins from him. Swaying, Wade watched them ride away with never a backward glance.

Now it was over, and with its ending seemed to go the remainder of Wade's strength. He felt himself growing dizzy, felt himself falling.

Then Kellman was kneeling in the mud beside him. "Wade, where'd they get you?"

"Shoulder. Ribs broke, I guess. They're gone?"

"Yeah. But we'll get 'em." He turned to yell at his men.

Wade caught his sleeve. "Let them go. They won't bother you again."

"No, by Judas! They need to be taught. . . ."

Wade's voice grew stronger momentarily. "Damn you, I said you'd do as I told you!"

Suddenly Kellman grinned. And shrugged. "All right. You're the boss." He stood and yelled in his bull voice: "Boys, come on back! Let 'em go!"

There was a period of darkness then for Wade, and a period of painful, interminable jolting in the buckboard. A period of vague awareness of Ginny's soft hands and softer voice.

But later he came out of the darkness and found himself in bed at the K Diamond. Ginny sat beside him, watching his face. Her expression was strange and unreadable.

Wade said: "I killed Curt. You hate me for that."

She shook her head.

"But you'll be leaving?"

She shrugged dispiritedly. "Why does that matter to you? You have Ellen."

Wade smiled. "I never had her. I only thought I did."

Ginny nodded soberly. "And I've decided that I never had Curt, either."

Wade groped for her hand. He said: "Stick around a while. Let me get well enough to give you an argument about leaving. Will you promise me that?"

He saw her nod and he felt her hand's pressure. And he knew that now everything would be all right.

ABOUT THE AUTHOR

Lewis B. Patten wrote more than ninety Western novels in thirty years, and three of them won Spur Awards from the Western Writers of America, and the author received the Golden Saddleman Award. Indeed, this points up the most remarkable aspect of his work: not that there is so much of it, but that so much of it is so fine. Patten was born in Denver, Colorado, and served in the U.S. Navy, 1933–1937. He was educated at the University of Denver during the war years and became an auditor for the Colorado Department of Revenue during the 1940s. It was in this period that he began contributing significantly to Western pulp magazines, fiction that was from the beginning fresh and unique and revealed Patten's lifelong concern with the sociological and psychological affects of group psychology on the frontier. He became a professional writer at the time of his first novel, *Massacre at White River* (1952). The dominant theme in much of his fiction is the notion of justice, and its opposite, injustice. In his first novel it has to do with exploitation of the Ute Indians, but as he matured as a writer he explored this theme with significant and poignant detail in small towns throughout the early West. Crimes, such as rape or lynching, are often at the center of his stories. When the values embodied in these small towns are examined closely, they are found to be wanting. Conformity is always easier than taking a stand. Yet, in Patten's view of the American West, there is usually a man or a woman who refuses to conform. Among his finest titles, always a difficult choice, are surely *Death of a Gunfighter* (1968), *A Death in Indian Wells* (1970), and *The Law at Cottonwood* (1978). No less noteworthy are his previous Five Star Westerns, *Tincup in the Storm Country, Trail to Vicksburg, Death Rides the Denver Stage, The Woman at Ox-Yoke,* and *Ride the Red Trail.* His next Five Star Western will be *Montana Gunfighter.*